Shiny Pippin
and the
Impossible Door

Harry Heape

Illustrated by
Rebecca Bagley

90 YEARS OF EXCELLENCE
FABER & FABER

First published in 2019
by Faber and Faber Limited
Bloomsbury House, 74–77 Great Russell Street,
London WC1B 3DA

Typeset in Caslon by M Rules
Printed and bound by
CPI Group (UK) Ltd, Croydon CR0 4YY

A CIP record for this book
is available from the British Library

ISBN 978–0–571–33219–9

FSC
www.fsc.org
MIX
Paper from
responsible sources
FSC® C101712

1 3 5 7 9 10 8 6 4 2

'A perfect gift for all those 6 & 7 year olds, **a guaranteed hit!**'

Theo, age 6

'Children who enjoy **David Walliams** are likely to be enthralled.'

Children's Books Ireland

'A truly magical book. We have found a new favourite author and **cannot wait for his next book.**'

Polly, age 8

'A funny, splendid book filled with adventure and friendship.'

Kacper, age 9

'I read it to my sons and **we laughed ourselves inside out.**'
Ed Byrne

'**I recommend it** for anyone that likes magical, detective and exciting stories.'

Freya, age 8

All children's reviews provided by Toppsta

HARRY HEAPE is an artist, a visionary and a very successful none-of-your-businessman. A shy and quiet man, Harry lives and writes on the edge of a magical forest where he spends any spare time that he has collecting pine cones and volunteering at his local monkey prison.

REBECCA BAGLEY lives in Bath (the city, not A BATH, although she did have one once) where she draws pictures so she doesn't have to get a real job. When she's not hanging out in the world of children's books, she'll probably be in a headstand, plotting how to best smuggle a husky into her flat without anyone noticing.

For Isolde, Sonny, Matt and Ione,

with all my love.

HH

x

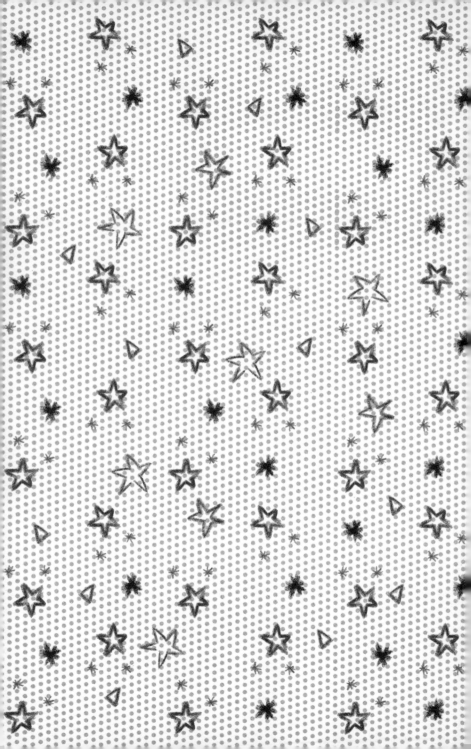

Twinkle, Twinkle, Little Star

A note from Sir Harold of Heape, author and underwater disco-dancing champion.

Remember the prologue, my lovely lovely book muffins? The bit where we hear about the magical star and I give you more little sections of slimportant funformation?

(Reader's voice) *Oh yes, it's mostly the same, so we just skip it and jump to Chapter One.*

Gaah! Are you kidding me? YOU SKIP IT? I've a jolly good mind to telephone the book police and have you locked up in word jail. You must read the prologue as carefully as a cockroach because the funformation this time is even more dreamy, slimportant and funusual.

Check it.

One hundred years ago, high in the night sky, a little old star flew through a distant galaxy. It was a brilliant star, the most fantastic in the whole sky, a star bursting with *magical possibilities*.

The star was ten trillion years old and it knew that it was dying. It arced between planets and in and out of comets for a year and a day until it was no bigger than a cauliflower.

It wanted somewhere beautiful to die, somewhere where it could pass on its magic. Finally, it spotted our little blue planet, and it felt instinctively that this was the perfect place.

It hurtled towards the ground, intent on crashing into a hillside and burying its powers deep within the soil. A farmer saying goodnight to his animals watched it descend above his home.

A travelling circus had made its home on the edge of the town. Very close by, the little star knew it wouldn't make the ground, and so it self-destructed and exploded in a shower of very special, shimmering sparkles, which rained down on the hillsides, the circus, the surrounding forest, and down into an old mine shaft.

The sparkles rained down on the farmer's little cottage, where his young family slept. They drifted down its chimney where they fizzed and flickered and buzzed and bounced through all the rooms.

A mother slept, with her twin babies, a little girl and a little boy, in a crib beside the bed, as the magic danced through their home. As they slumbered, incredible things began to happen all around them. A group of sparkles picked up a pen on the bedside table and began to write a note that the mother would find in the morning.

This starry note was cryptic and crucial, and the mother would keep it on her at all times, eventually passing it on to her children. It was written in rhyme and told of magic, mystery and a myriad of possibilities. It spoke of locks and keys and gold and gateways to strange lands and we shall hear much more about this note as our adventure progresses.

As the sparkles danced and the family slept, high in the star-strewn sky, something colossal was circling the earth – a FAR, FAR BIGGER star than the one which had just exploded above the forest. This star was **a thousand times** the size, and it hurtled through the night sky towards our little blue planet. This enormous star was far too big to crash into the ground, and so it orbited the earth high in the sky, zooming around and around Planet Earth, trying to find somewhere safe to land.

Eventually it spotted an island in the middle of the ocean and, at its centre, a volcano. This would be the safest place for it to come down. It plummeted into the centre of the volcano, which erupted and spewed magical sparkly stardust over the entire island. A hundred years later, all of this twinkly, shiny, brilliant magic from both stars had grown into something rather wonderful and this, my lovely readers, is what our stories are all about.

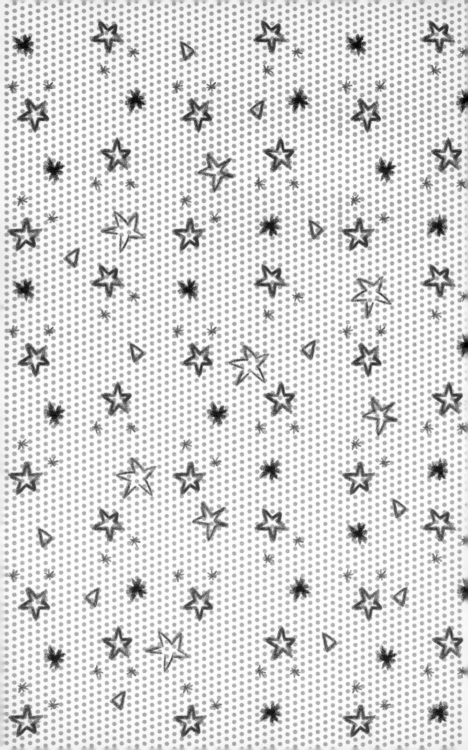

Granny's
Garden House

Woo-hoo! I have been waiting ages for you. Yes, YOU! And you, and you, and you, and especially you!

All my tickly book muffins are back again which makes me so happy that I want to shout, 'Honk-a-doodle-yee-ha,' and break into a smooth little dance where I pretend to go deep-sea diving underwater, shaking my hips, and holding my nose. THAT'S how very excited I am.

You see, the thing is, I am buzzing like a bee on his birthday about this next story because everything goes as wonky as a donkey and gets extremely funusual, and I'm not even kidneying.

I'm itching like the bum-bum of a baboon to get started on the next Shiny Pippin badventure, SHINY PIPPIN AND THE IMPOSSIBLE DOOR! Now that you are all here, we must do that immediately because there is such an awful lot to tell.

You will of course remember that the H to the E to the R to the O of our stories is a magical little girl called Pippin. She spends a lot of time hanging out with her awesome granny. Pippin and her granny are Shiny, which means that they can talk to Shiny animals, and they share a very special telepathy with these animals too. Shiny animals are animals that have the same magic, a magic that came from a very special star more than a hundred years ago. If you are a police dog having this as your bedtime story, then the magic came from a very special star more than SEVEN HUNDRED years ago.

I can give you more reminderoonys later about other sections of slimportant funformation as we gallop through the story, but I'm not going to dwell on that now because what I really want to do is get ~~farted~~ (*pardon me*) started.

The first thing to do is to find out what Pippin is up to, because EVERYTHING starts and finishes with this magical little mega muffin.

Down outside Granny's little cottage in the woods, it was morning time. Soft sunlight filtered through the trees and made Pippin feel happy and nice about the

world. She was up and out of bed already because it was such a beautiful day. She was playing with Tony, her dearly beloved pet mouse and Shiny soulmate. They had already played three of their favourite games:

1) Battle Cheese Galactica
2) Urgent Speed Crisps
3) Hunt the Hazelnut

It was still early and they had just enough time for a game of hide-and-sleep before breakfast, so this is what they were doing right now in the garden outside Granny's cottage on the edge of the magical forest.

Pippin had her eyes closed and her head against the trunk of an apple tree. She was counting while Tony the mouse was finding somewhere cool to hide and go to sleep.

'Ninety-seven, ninety-eight, ninety-nine, ONE HUNDRED THOUSAND! Coming, ready or not,' she shouted.

Our little friend set off around the garden that surrounded Granny's cottage. She looked in the wood store. Tony was not there. She looked in the greenhouse. Tony was not there either. She looked in the outside toilet.

'**Gaaah!!!!!!** Sorry, Granny!' said Pippin, blushing. 'You should lock the door! I didn't know you were having a private moment!'

'Don't worry, my little dumpling, I won't say anything if you don't!' Granny giggled with a magical twinkle. 'If you are looking for that adorable little mouse of yours, I saw him scuttle past the back door as I was heading here for my morning plo—'

'**Gaaah!!!!!**' Pippin screamed for a second time and flew off towards

the back garden before her granny could finish the rest of THAT sentence, thank you very much.

At the back of the house Pippin scanned the area, pretending she was an amazing search droid called FINDY STUFF 5000.

FINDY STUFF 5000 clicked into SEARCH MODE and looked:

1.0) In the milk bottles that were on the back step

2.0) Inside Granny's watering can

3.0) Under Granny's sun hat, which was on a bench

DOWNLOAD COMPLETE: NO TONY

Pippin scratched her head and rubbed her pretend-robot tummy, which helped her reboot, and as she did so, she started to feel magic twinkles coursing through her pretend-electric bones. She recognised this yummy feeling. It was the start of a lovely Shine. It was with Tony and the little girl began slowly to listen in on the little mouse to see where he might be. She felt as though he was hiding somewhere dark, she felt as though she could smell the strong sniffage of wood, lawn mowers, deckchairs, and . . . sniff, sniff, sniff . . . barbecue charcoal.

Looking up, she immediately spotted where the little mouse was. He had to be in what Granny called her garden house. Now, I'm not going to lie to you because *friends don't lie*, this wasn't really a house at all, it was just a little shed that backed onto a wall at the end of Granny's garden. Pippin smiled, and as she did so, the twinkly Shine popped like a wobbly bubble and she raced towards the small garden-house shed.

Opening the stiff wooden door as quietly as she could, Pippin saw a shedload of stuff – she saw bikes and shelves and brushes and spades and an old barbecue and a cockerel in a cowboy hat.

Haha, not really a cockerel in a cowboy

hat, that was just me messing about like a big NINNY to see if you were listening, and you were. Lovely.

So, stepping silently inside, Pippin peered into jam jars and behind tins of paint, and inside old plant pots. Still no Tony Macaroni.

She looked inside tins and behind candlesticks and on the shelves that stood along one wall of the shed. No Tony. She looked behind deckchairs and on ledges and behind the little curtains that Granny had hung at the windows. Still. No. Tony.

She listened very carefully for little

rustling noises that might give away Tony's hiding place, and then suddenly she heard the faint but unmistakable sound of her little mouse singing a song. Tony was so confident of not being found that he was releasing a nice relaxing nut-based ballad to himself and it went a little bit like this.

(Now, the rule of the last book was that any grown-up reading this aloud must sing – or pay twenty pence into your piggy bank. Because everything is now more expensive, I have put the fee up for this book to twenty-five pence. This is called inflation.)

Sing:

'Ten hazelnuts sitting in my
    bowl,
Ten hazelnuts sitting in my
    bowl,
And if one hazelnut should
    accidentally fall (into my big
    soft tummy)
There'd be nine hazelnuts sitting
    in my bowl.

'Nine hazelnuts sitting in my bowl,
Nine hazelnuts sitting in my
    bowl,

And if one hazelnut should
accidentally fall (into my big
soft tummy)
There'd be eight hazelnuts sitting
in my bowl.'

Pippin crept towards the sound of the singing, which was coming from the back wall of the shed. This wall was covered with an old heavy patchwork quilt, which had been hung there to make the garden house look homely and pretty. Pippin inched forward quietly, planning to surprise Tony. As she tiptoed closer, she smiled – little Tony had no idea that he was about to be busted!

'Eight hazelnuts sitting in my bowl,
Eight hazelnuts sitting in my bowl,
And if one hazelnut should
   accidentally fall (into my big
   soft tummy)
There'd be seven hazelnuts sitting
   in my bowl—'

Pippin reached up and grabbed the side of the quilt. She pulled it back, quick as a flash, fully expecting to see little Tony and his fluffy belly singing away. But this is NOT what she saw at all.

What she did see made her stop dead in her tracks and gasp. Behind the quilt was a large oak door – the kind of doorway that you might see in an ancient freaky castle, a tricky temple, or a wiggly old church.

Honk-a-doodle-flipsters, my lovely friends! I do not know what to think about this because it is so confusnig— I MEAN CONFUSING! I don't know where to start trying to explain why there was a huge funusual door, which looked like it was from a chuffing castle, in Granny's wonky little shed.

This door was absurd, preposterous, inconceivable – in fact IT WAS IMPOSSIBLE. This door was so totally out of the question that when I heard about it, I just had to make it the title of this book. It made me feel very excited because, my lovely friends, magic like this does not come along very often and, as such, it is extremely special.

Back to the story, which is in no way snorey . . .

Goodness gracious jinkies and honk-a-doodle-crumpets. How funusual is that? thought Pippin to herself.

To help us visualise this completely unacceptable door, I have asked my great friend and picture wizard, Lady Babecca of Raggley, to draw the door especially for us with one of her most enchanted felt-tip pens.

Check it.

This was spookier than five foggy forests
in February. What on earth was going on?

Where did the door lead to? Pippin began to feel so anxious that she had to sing a little song about feeling very nervous. Anyone who is also feeling like Pippin can of course be let off the twenty-five pence singing rule.

> *'If you're anxious and you know it*
> *clasp your hands.*
> *If you're anxious and you know it*
> *clasp your hands.'*

She remembered losing Tony in a previous badventure and it had made her feel sadder than a kitten in a cage. Where was her little mouse?

She banged on the doors with her fists.

'TONY! Are you in there? Tony! I give up. You win. Come out, Tony, I am feeling very worried!'

Suddenly Tony's cute little head popped out of the keyhole! 'Yay! I win,' he said.

With a huge sigh of relief, Pippin snatched up her friend, placed him gently into her pocket and clutched him to her beating heart. 'Phew,' she said. 'I was worried for a second.'

Looking at the old wooden door she began to calm

down. 'What . . . is . . . in . . . there . . . Tony?' she asked.

'Nothing,' said the little mouse, rather matter-of-factly. 'A room or something, maybe some stairs. I didn't really look. I just hid in there and did two walnutty farts and some singing,' he continued.

Pippin pulled a torch out of her pocket and shone it through the keyhole. There did seem to be a room or hallway of some sort, but this couldn't be. Granny's shed BACKED ON TO A WALL. This door couldn't lead anywhere because of the wall, but the problem was that IT DID LEAD SOMEWHERE. Impossible.

To make sure that she was not going mad, Pippin walked out of the shed and around to the back of it. It was as she thought – the wooden wall of the shed was right up against the wall of Granny's garden. Pippin could fit her arm into the gap but that was all. She peeped over the wall to see if there was anything unusual but there was just a field. A field she had seen a thousand times.

With her mind whirring, like a none-of-your-businessman who'd lost his best briefcase, and feeling very excited, Pippin rushed inside to ask her granny all about the impossible door because it felt important and it felt unreal and it felt to our hero like the most mysterious thing that she had ever seen.

A Letter to
My Readers

Dearest Dusty Bookgobblers,

I am writing you a letter for this part of the story because I need to convey to you some slimportant funformation about evil Doctor Blowfart, the baddie of our stories.

Sometimes, when your slimformation is VERY funportant, it is good to put it in a letter so that it doesn't go MIA or AWOL.

(Reader's voice) *Harry, you big nonsense man, I don't know what MIA or AWOL mean!*

Ah. Sozzikins. They are dippy army words which mean 'missing in action' and 'absent without leave', so they both basically mean MISSING.

Back to the letter, which contains important information that must not go MIA or AWOL or MISSING.

I need you to know that right at the very moment Pippin was nonsensing around in the garden outside her granny's house, Doctor

Blowfart was up to extreme naughtiness hundreds of miles away.

The enormous science stinker was in a room which looked just like a blacksmith's forge. On a large metal table in the middle of the room was a huge pile of papers and plans all about something rotten that the mean old goat was about to do.

Also on the table was a little silver bell. The Doctor rang the bell and within a second, as if from nowhere, two well-dressed monkeys appeared. One wore a cowboy hat, the other a fez. The Doctor drew them close to him and whispered terrible plans and frightful tricks, pointing out things on the papers that lay scattered around on the desk. The monkeys nodded as the Doctor explained exactly what he needed them to do.

'Do you understand?' the Doctor asked, finally.

'Yes, my master,' the monkeys replied as one.

'It will be like taking candy from a baby,' replied the monkey in the cowboy hat.

'Excellent,' whispered the Doctor. 'Then be gone and do not return without it.'

I am sorry to make you read this letter so early on in our story. I hope that reading about the beastly Doctor hasn't put you off this story altogether. I cannot make it better by telling you some nice things because a VIP is about to arrive at my house. By VIP I don't mean a very important person. I mean a very important pee. When you gotta go, you gotta go.

See you in the next chappy-wappy-wapter (after I wuddle off for a widdle).

Fondest regards,

Harry Heape

Harry Heape

Author

Guess What. Guess What. Guess What. Guess What. Guess What?!

Back at Granny's, Pippin felt as though a fat new mysterious mystery had just mysteriously landed in her lap. Our favourite silver-haired old lady had finished her VERY IMPORTANT BUSINESS and was just going back into the house when Pippin arrived, skidding around the corner as if she was in a cartoon. 'Granny, Granny!' she shouted excitedly, 'I have found something that is very mysterious and strange in your garden house. IT IS VERY MYSTERIOUS AND STRANGE INDEED.'

'Well, that sounds funusual and exciting,' beamed Granny. 'Let's go inside and put some marshmallows into our cakeholes, and you can tell me all about it,' she twinkled.

Just as our little hero was about launch

into a big old babble of questions for her granny, they both heard the roar of an enormous motor vehicle. Pippin grinned as she saw her friend Mungo screech around the corner in his fabulous fire engine which he had converted into a nice-cream van. This almost certainly meant a morning Magnum or a scrumptious Cornetto for Pippin and her granny.

They could both tell that Mungo was in a massive rush – he must have driven in a real hurry because his ice-cream fire engine was so zonked that it looked as if it was panting like a big friendly worn-out sheepdog in the soft morning sunshine.

Mungo leaped out of the nice-cream van like a legend, bursting with huge amounts of funergy and excitement.

'GUESS WHAT? GUESS WHAT? GUESS WHAT? GUESS WHAT? GUESS WHAT!?'

'Have you won a new pair of spotty underpants in a competition?' said Granny, looking over her spectacles and wrinkling her nose.

'Better than that!' said Mungo.

'Have you invented a wicked new ice cream that makes you burp sparkles?'

said Pippin, joining in with the lovely funusual nonsense.

'Better even than that!' replied Mungo. 'I'll tell you,' he beamed. 'There is to be a huge ceremony in the town hall FOR ME! I am being presented with a massive new and wicked gold chain because . . .

THEY ARE MAKING ME MAYOR OF FUNSPRINGS!'

Pippin jumped up and down and clapped and shouted, 'YAY for Mayor Mungo! YAY for Mayor Mungo! YAY for Mayor

Mungo!' She felt so happy for her friend that she did a fartwheel, which is a cross between a cartwheel and a you-know-what.

'Oh, that's wonderful news!' said Granny, smiling. She knew this was something that Mungo had been wishing for, for a very long time. 'When is this huge ceremony to be?' the old lady asked, thinking that she would write it on the calendar, and maybe buy a new dress for the occasion.

'It's in fifteen minutes,' said Mungo looking rather sheepish. 'I had a big pile of snorey boring letters, which I had not been opening, and when I did and finally got to the last one, it was my special guest of honour invite to my ceremony.'

'Well, in that case we don't have a moment to lose,' said lovely, twinkly Granny, who really was a muffin. Quick as a quarter of a flash, they all jumped into the Mungomobile and zoomed off towards town. As they sped away from Granny's cottage, Pippin looked over her shoulder and caught a glimpse of the garden-house shed.

'Granny,' said Pippin, alive with excitement as the nice-cream van roared around the first corner. 'I MUST tell you about what I found in your shed!'

'I am SO SAD that Rosemary and

George are away,' Mungo interrupted.

For those of you that need another reminderoony: Rosemary was Lady Elliot, Mungo's splendid new wife, and George was her little boy.

'Where are they?' asked Pippin, forgetting for a moment about the shed and the impossible door.

'Oh, they're just on one of their WEEKENDS AWAY,' said Mungo with a grin. Everybody knew what a WEEKEND AWAY meant for these two because Rosemary had a secret life: she was in fact none other than The Dagger, a mysterious and elusive international jewellery thief. She was training George to follow her into the family naughty business, so they were probably stealing the crown jewels or breaking into a big posh bank in order to make off with a sack of rich people's diamonds that they would then give to the poor.

'Oh, that's too bad,' said Granny. 'But at least you will have us there to cheer you on when you make your speech,' she said, wrinkling her small and adorable nose for the second time.

'MY WHAT?' blurted a very surprised Mungo, almost swerving off the road.

'Your speech,' replied Granny. 'You will need to say a few thank yous. Just be yourself. What can go wrong?' she added with a smile directed at her granddaughter.

Trying not to laugh, Pippin chipped in. 'I shall send a Shine to the forest in the hope that some of your animal fans can come and join us in seeing you receive your mayor's chunky golden necklace.'

'Thanks,' said Mungo, frowning to himself. He had never been very good at talking in front of people because he always got very nervowonky and then sometimes got his WORDS IN THE ORDER WRONG, IF YOU MEAN WHAT I KNOW.

Before very long, they were driving down Babbins Wood Road and into the beautiful town of Funsprings. At the bottom of the hill, they turned right onto Armpit Avenue and pulled up outside the town hall, where people were gathering for the big event.

Mungo dashed inside through the crowds to get himself ready for the presentation, leaving Granny and Pippin inside the nice-cream van. It was good for Pippin to see the big man so happy. She thought that he had been a bit sad recently. She wondered if it was because Mungo so desperately wished to be Shiny too. Imagine you had a big gang of friends and they all spoke a different language and you couldn't understand them – it *would* make you sad.

Alone with her granny, Pippin seized the opportunity and blurted out all that had happened that morning – about the hide-and-sleep and the Shine which led her to the shed, and Tony's singing, and the quilt, and finally the impossible door.

When she had quite finished, little Granny looked at little Pippin.

'I believe that you have made an incredibly important discovery, my love. What you have discovered may be something that my brother Edward and I started looking for more than fifty years ago.'

Reminderoony time. Edward was Granny's twin brother. He also had the gift of Shining. But something terrible happened to Edward when he was a young man – he lost his Shiny soulmate, a cat called Jean. Edward never recovered. His heart was broken and his Shiny magic took on a very dark tone. Striking off on his own, away from his family, he began doing bad things. Edward became the evil Doctor Blowfart. As you probably know, Pippin, Granny and their woodland anipals had all been through several scary badventures with Doctor Blowfart in the past.

'But you must have known the door was in your shed, Granny?' Pippin asked, wide-eyed. 'You must have seen it when you hung up that old quilt?'

'No, I didn't see the door, my love,' Granny answered. 'It wasn't there.' Pippin's mouth popped open in amazement, as her granny continued. 'There is Shiny magic at work in this world, my dear, magic that is

WAY BIGGER than

you and I being able to talk to animals.'

Pippin's eyes grew to the size of saucers.

How could there be a bigger magic than

Shining? she thought to herself.

'There is so much I need to tell to you,'

said Granny. 'Everything I know begins

with an ancient prophecy that was handed

down to me by my mother – your great

grandmother. It was written on a note on

her bedside table by someone or something

the very night that the star landed in the

hills around Funsprings.

A bigger magic than Shining! An ancient

prophecy! Which appeared mysteriously next to the bed of her great grandmother! Pippin was transfixed – this was amazoinks, funusual, and incredibubble. 'Go on,' she gently urged, urgently.

Granny continued, almost in a whisper. Pippin had to lean forward so she didn't miss a single word. 'When Edward and I were young, we copied down my mother's note, the prophecy. I have carried a copy everywhere with me ever since.' Granny pulled out a tattered old envelope from her breast pocket and produced an ancient, yellowing piece of paper.

This document is so slimportant to our

story, I need help to show you fizzactly what it looks like, so . . .

Calling Rebecca Wiggley.

Repeat.

Calling Rebecca Wiggley.

Crack out your magic felt-tips once more.

Over.

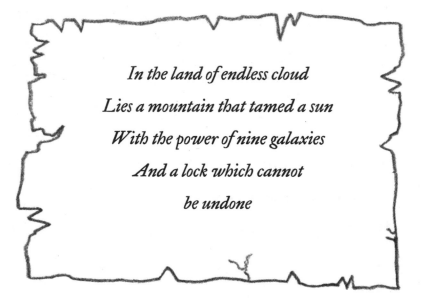

In the land of endless cloud
Lies a mountain that tamed a sun
With the power of nine galaxies
And a lock which cannot
be undone

By a simple key for the upstairs-

upstairs you will need

Golden drops one, two, three

For two of the gifted there must be

Through four gateways

tread carefully

To Everywhere, Adventure

& Eternity

And one more to bring you home

Pippin read it over and over again. It didn't seem to make much sense. 'Mmm,' she pondered, 'it is so riddley and funusual,' she said.

'I know!' said Granny. 'I have been trying to work it out for most of my life.'

Just at that moment, there was a tiny thud on the windscreen of the nice-cream van as their little friend, Oddplop the frog, landed. Then Pippin saw that one of Mungo's favourite animal friends, Snape the little lamb, had also arrived to lend support.

Granny and Pippin climbed out of the nice-cream van and began to make their way into the town hall. Our little hero was frustrated – she wanted to begin investigating the mystery now, now, now, now, now, now, now, but she couldn't. It was time for Mungo's big presentation.

Mysterious prophecies and magical gladventures would just have to wait. What Pippin didn't know, though, was that she would not have to wait very long at all . . . Hurtling through the sky towards them were a couple of very naughty somethings that would turn their universe upside down, and set them off on an adventure which would be totally

OUT OF THIS WORLD.

Mayor Mungo's
Magical Moment

Pippin and Granny squeezed into
the busy hall, with Snape and
Tony and Oddplop in tow. It was
a huge light and airy room, and it was full
of people. At one end were big glass floor-
to-ceiling windows, which overlooked

the river and the town beyond. Our gang edged their way through the crowds, towards the small stage at the front of the hall.

You will be very glad to hear that I am not going to tell you every detail about the ceremony. That would be WAY TOO SNOREY for a book such as this one.

This book, as you well know, is a banging adventure book. It is the kind of book where things like this could happen:

...

1) Battling evil scientists on top of fast-moving trains in the mountains. **BOOM**

2) Flying out of exploding buildings on zip wires and landing on supersonic skateboards. *POW*

3) Shooting flaming arrows over castle walls before storming in and rescuing a wet prince from a mean ogre.

OUCH THAT REALLY HURT.

The ceremony droned on in a sea of snorey-borey adult chitter-chatter. This is what it sounded like to Pippin:

'Blah, blah, blah, blah it gives me great pleasure, blah blah.

'Blah blah, new mayor, Mungo blah blah.

'Blah blah present to him blah blah blah, a brand-new mayoral chain made with gold freshly mined from beneath Funsprings itself.'

This last bit made Pippin sit up and take notice! She had been into the mines around Funsprings in one of her earlier badventures. Also, she loved gold because it was so golden and exciting and it made her think of adventure and Tutankhamun and a pirate's treasure. The chain was not a disappointment. It was so fat and so shiny that it seemed to light up Mungo's big happy face as he wore it.

At last the boring ceremony was over. Everybody cheered, and the band played a joyous tune as Mungo left the stage and went off into a little back room wearing his new chain.

'Let's go and cuddle a mayor!' said Granny, twinkling like twenty-two trumpets and twelve trombones. And they all dashed and trotted backstage to say 'well done' to their most favouritest Mungo, who had indeed done well.

'Yay for Mayor Mungo!' beamed Pippin, bouncing into the room.

'Confabulations!' said Granny, following behind. Snape the little lamb baahed cheekily. 'And a well done from meeeee, you biiiig hairy baboooooon', she added, knowing there was no way Mungo would understand, not being Shiny.

Mungo spun round and looked as though he had seen a ghost. 'What did you say?' he blurted, looking down at the little lamb. It was now Snape's turn to feel very surprised, because, for the first time, she could understand what the big man was saying. 'Err . . . well done from meeeee . . .' the little lamb baaahed quietly.

Mungo danced up and down with joy. 'This is the greatest present in the universe. I can understand you! I can understand you!! I can understand you!!!' he laughed, picking up Snape for a delicious, woolly snuggle.

Granny and Pippin stood open-mouthed with amazement. They were both quite used to being Shiners and being able to communicate with Shiny animals. But now, somehow, as if by magic, Mungo was Shining too! Pippin and Granny were

SOOOOOooooooo happy. They knew what this would mean for him.

'I too can understand you, *amigo*,' said Oddplop the frog from up on Granny's shoulder.

'Woo-hoo. Me too,' said little Tony, popping his head out of Pippin's pocket. 'And by the way, your farts smell of roast beef and Cornettos,' added the little mouse.

Mungo was now officially the happiest man in the world. Tears of joy trickled down his face as he began chatting away to all the animals, knowing they had an awful lot of catching up to do.

'Please can I try on your lovely golden

mayor chain?' asked Pippin, interrupting.

'Sure,' said the big man and he lifted it off as the little lamb carried on with her adorable chatting.

But when the chain was off, something terribubble happened. Mungo found that he was no longer able to funderstand the little lamb! Oh dearie meatballs. It was exactly like that moment in a game of pass the parcel when the music stops and you are just about to pass the parcel but haven't quite handed it over.

Mungo looked at the chain in his hands, and then put it back over his head. Amazing. He could understand all of Snape's woolly words once more.

'It is my new mayoral chain that is making me Shiny!'

Granny understood in a second what was going on. 'It must be because of the gold from beneath Funsprings,' she said to Mungo, and the big man looked as happy as a pig in funnyland.

'This is the most wonderful present in the world,' said Mungo to his friends. I shall wear it always, and I will protect it with my life. He was interrupted by a knock at the door. It was the town's wealthy none-of-your-businessman, Sir Aslan Ragu.

'People are very keen to welcome the town's new mayor and hear his speech!' he said. 'But first it's time to come and shake a few hands and pose for some photographs,' he added.

Mungo beamed. He already L-O-V-E-D loved being Mayor. 'Come on, Snape, you woolly little muffin, it's photo time.'

Snape baahed back in bleat, the international language of sheep, 'I aaam only going to be in a phoe-toe with you if you bring me some yummy graaaasssss to eat. Understaaaaand?' And Mungo grinned and said, 'Okay!' because he did understaaaaand – he underststoooooood every last word the little lamb was saying.

A few moments later, back in the hall, the new Mayor was working his way through the crowds, shaking hands with babies and patting grown-ups on the head.

Pippin sat on the edge of the stage, swinging her feet and sighing, because this kind of waiting around was no fun for a little girl who craved adventure. As she gazed out of the big glass windows at the end of the room, she noticed something strange high up in the sky.

It looked as though a tiny storm cloud was heading towards them from up in the heavens. It was a dark cloud, which swirled this way and that, kicking and punching its way past the rest of the clouds in its path. Pippin Shined to Granny over on the other side of the room, and she immediately looked up at the sky.

The fighting ball of cloud was like an

angry tornado or a dark and brooding meteor, and it was getting closer and closer, heading directly towards them.

Pippin covered her head with her hands, but the window did not shatter. Instead, just for a moment, the glass seemed to turn to liquid, like bubble mixture, and the cloud squelched into the room and tumbled along the floor. In a moment, the cloud disappeared and out stepped a pair of extremely sharp-looking, very well-dressed monkeys.

Pippin and Granny recognised them immediately – they were the ghost monkeys who had worked with Blowfart in their last adventure, but this time they were as real as you and me.

You have to see them, my lovely book-gobbling friends – THIS is what the terrible ghost monkeys looked like. Take it away, picture wizard R to the B . . .

One monkey threw bananas into each

corner of the room, while the other stole a trombone from the band and began to play. The bananas exploded, letting off smoke and glitter and sparkles, and the room was complete and utter monkey mayhem.

People ran, screaming and shouting, as the monkeys wreaked havoc and the whole scene descended into a mass of smoke, trombone music and swirling, glittery pandemonium.

The monkey in the fez took a microphone from the stage and began to sing as they scattered anarchy all around the room.

(Twenty-five pence if you don't sing.)

Two little monkeys jumping
  on the bed,
One fell down and bumped his head,
Mama called the doctor and the
  doctor said,
No more monkey business jumping
  on the bed.

They danced and they sang, and the room filled up with smoke so nobody could see anything that was going on.

AND THEN, AS QUICKLY AS IT HAD STARTED, IT WAS OVER.

The smoke cleared and the monkeys, as if by magic, were GONE. In the deafening silence, Pippin looked across the devastated room, past upturned tables and broken chairs, and then she spotted her friend Mungo clutching Snape protectively to his chest.

In a flash, both Pippin and Mungo realised a terribubble thing had happened: Mungo's magical new chain – which had turned him Shiny and made him the happiest man alive – was MIA missing, AWOL, GONE.

The big man let out an anguished cry. Snape baahed and bleated but poor Mungo could no longer understand her and began to cry. He'd been given the gift of Shining, only for it to be cruelly snatched away by the monkey burglars. This was the worst thing that could have happened to him. Pippin looked across the room at the big man and saw a colossal sadness etched all over her dear friend's face.

Cloud Chasers

Granny and the gang gathered ~~immediaterly~~ ~~immoodiataly~~ as quickly as shmickly pickly, for there wasn't a moment to lose. Rushing outside, clever Pippin looked up into the sky. 'There!' she shouted and pointed. High up, over the hill, in the late afternoon sky, was the fighting, tumbling dark cloud of monkey mayhem, which had, minutes earlier, wrought such havoc inside the town hall.

Mungo dearly wanted his magical chain back and rushed around like a man possessed. 'Quick, to the Mungomobile!' he urged, and in a third of moment, or mo for short, they were all inside. He fired up the engine and reversed at high speed along the full length of Armpit Avenue, before roaring up the hill and out of town in pursuit of the thieves that had stolen his magical chain and his happiness.

Oblivious to all that had gone on in the

town hall, little Tony was still snoozing in Pippin's pocket, having the most terrific dream about living in a hazelnut house on the side of a mountain made entirely of Cheddar. No such luck for Pippin – she was in the centre of the action and leaned out of the open window, craning her neck to see if she could see the writhing cloud of monkey bad.

'I got it!' she said. 'But I just really wish I had a—' Granny passed her a pair of binoculars. 'You read my mind,' grinned the little girl. 'These make things a lot easier.'

Our hero kept a careful eye on the cloud, giving Mungo directions so that he

could follow it from the ground. Every now and then, the big man would lean out of the window, shaking his fist and shouting things like:

'Gaaah, give me back my chain, you thieving monkeys!!!'

'Monkeys! You are messing with the wrong mayor!'

And 'Why, you little . . . Why, I oughta . . . Why, you sons of a gun!'

For miles and miles they wound their way along the tops of the moors, beneath a leaden sky. The landscape was bleak and dramatic with nothing but grey grass and the occasional craggy crow perched on a wall. From time to time, the road would dip downhill and take them into gloomy little towns with names like Darkscar, Longwall and Slack Bottom.

Pippin kept her focus on the rumbling monkey cloud up in the heavens. The team knew they were on the right track as they kept spotting banana skins on gateposts, in bushes and in trees. One had even landed on an old man's head as he stood waiting at a village bus stop.

Eventually Granny pointed out

something in the distance. 'Look!' the old lady exclaimed. 'It's the sea!' And sure enough, there it was – the big beautiful grey-blue ocean. It is a wonderful feeling to see the sea when you are not expecting to. Mungo stopped feeling quite so desperate, just for a moment. He was tempted to run along the seashore, feel the spray of the waves and forget all his troubles.

Granny leaned in towards her beloved Pippin and whispered, 'Nothing's quite as adventurous as the ocean, is it, my dear?' For the first time in hours, Pippin took her gaze away from the malevolent monkey cloud and gazed out over the sea.

Through the open window of the Mungomobile, with the wind blowing back her hair, she imagined the mighty ocean frozen and how it would feel to skate at supersonic speed over its ice-covered waves, jumping and landing and skating all the way across the mighty slumbering sea to whatever strange and magical lands lay beyond.

As the freezing windy wind whipped Pippin's cheeks, she thought briefly about the impossible door in her granny's shed. That would just have to wait a day or two, she thought. There was more important work to do right now for her beloved friend Mungo.

Granny felt all of these thoughts Shining out of her granddaughter and smiled at how similar she and the little girl were becoming. Pippin's fantastical oceanic thought bubble popped as they screeched around the next corner. Our little hero remembered her important job, picked up the binoculars and homed in on the dark and menacing monkey cloud once more, her sharp mind alive with questions.

- How did they fly?
- How did they burst through glass as though it was made of bubble mixture?

✨🐚 What did they want with
Mungo's chain?

Outside it was suddenly turning quite
foggy and little Pippin saw the gurning
cloud alter direction and plummet down,
like a murmuration of shape-shifting
starlings, towards the ground and out
of sight.

It had looked very much as though the
cloud was heading towards the point at
which the sea met the land. As Mungo
careered around yet another corner, they
saw a signpost pointing down a steep lane
towards the coast.

GATACRE'S COVE

'Aha!' said Granny with a twinkle. 'Gatacre's Cove! I wondered if we might be heading here,' she added with a knowing smile. 'I chased Blowfart and these monkeys here once before but they gave me the slip when they reached the sea. The trail always went cold. I travelled up the coast and down, back inland and searched the whole town. It was as if they had vanished into thin air.'

It was now getting dark. It seemed, from the way the cloud had descended into the little seaside town, that the monkeys were hiding out and resting somewhere nearby. And so our heroes decided to drive down and do a little bit of evening-time snooping in the hope that they would come face to face with the ghost monkeys, seize back Mungo's magical chain, and then head home for digestive biscuits and marshmallows on the sofa. It was a nice thought . . .

Mungo drove his ice-cream fire engine carefully down the steep cobbled streets, past sleepy fisherwomen's cottages and parked by the harbour.

The Mungomobile was tired after such a

speedy cross-country chase and was very pleased to be having a rest with a beautiful view of the sea. It was so exhausted, it didn't even worry about being pooped on by any sneery seagulls.

I have been pooped on by a seagull, my dear friends, and the first thing that people ALWAYS tell you is that it's lucky to be pooped on by a bird, but I have news for those people . . .

IT IS NOT LUCKY AT ALL! IT IS YUCKY!

I would say that it is, in fact, frightfully UNLUCKY to have a white poop-bomb

91

of fish filth go splat on your best hat, thank you very much for asking. If anyone says to you that it is good luck to be pooped on by any kind of bird, you must phone a police dog and have those fools arrested.

Sorry, my friends, that little section brought back some difficult feelings for me, as you may have gathered. Back to the story . . .

Our team had already begun to sneak around town looking for clues to where those pesky monkeys could be hiding out. Mungo had his geologist's head torch on and kept lighting up all the weird and wonderful street names, some of which looked like this:

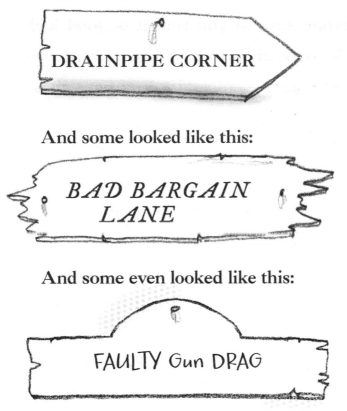

DRAINPIPE CORNER

And some looked like this:

BAD BARGAIN
LANE

And some even looked like this:

FAULTY Gun DRAG

Shiny Pippin, with Tony still fast asleep in her pocket, found hundroids and hundroids of banana skins but nothing more. Tired, worn out and with Mungo feeling very emotional, they found themselves standing under a lamp post outside an inn called the Boar's Head Hotel.

Granny could see that her gang had totally run out of funergy. 'Let's get a room for the night and start afresh in the morning,' she suggested. Nobody had any energy to even think about what else to do, so she pushed open the heavy oak door, which creaked very loudly indeed. As they all stepped inside, the busy chatter of the pub suddenly stopped and everyone turned and stared at them.

You could have cut the atmosphere with a knife. Oh dear. What did this strange place hold for our heroes? I will tell you tomorrow, because I need to go to bed just now I have to get up early in the morning to play badminton with my dear friend Samantha Dawn Glassbogey. She is terrific at badminton and I need all the rest I can get.

Goodnight.

Full Moon at the
Boar's Head Hotel

Our heroes stood just inside the doorway of the Boar's Head Hotel feeling very funwelcome. The feeling of their awkward arrival lasted just a moment until, from the bar, there came the shrill but very friendly voice of the landlady. 'Eeeeeeeeevening, strangers! What'll it be? Your usual?!'

Granny smiled at this welcoming lady and the gang walked gingerly towards her, and the pub regained its gentle chatter.

'Long way from home, my lovers?' said the nice landlady lady. 'I'm Nancy,' she added.

'Pleased to meet you,' replied Granny. 'We have had quite a day and would love a room for the night, if that is possible?'

'Of course. Follow me, my lovers, and I'll take you up. The little 'un must be exhausted,' she added, smiling down at Pippin.

Behind the bar was a row of hooks with two keys for each of the rooms – a key for the guests and a very slimportant spare key. The landlady grabbed one of the room keys, hitched up her pants, grinned, beckoned, and they followed, wearily, through a door to the side of the bar.

The landlady lady led them upstairs, past a snug little room, where some men were playing dominoes. There was an ancient visitors' book at the bottom of the stairs. Pippin paused and ran her fingers over the antique leather cover, wondering how many people had stayed in this ancient pub and what tales they would have been able to tell about their journey to this part of the world.

The kind landlady lady pointed out their nearest bathroom, in case anybody needed a wee in the widdle of the night, and then she showed our intrepid explorers into a warm and comfortable room. Within five minutes they'd climbed into their beds, exhausted after the day's mammoth monkey chase, and were snoring their heads off.

All except Pippin, who was wide awake because her mind was busy, busy, busy. It was another chance to think about the door in her granny's shed. The door her granny said she'd never seen before – which meant, thought Pippin, that it must have somehow just appeared. And then she remembered something that her granny had said earlier that day: *There is Shiny magic at work in this world, my dear, magic that is WAY BIGGER than you and I being able to talk to animals.'*

As her mind wandered, Pippin was gripped by a clever thought . . . her Granny had said that she'd chased Blowfart and the monkeys to this town before. If she had, then maybe Blowfart had stayed here. He could have signed the visitors' book! Perhaps there would be a comment written down which would help her understand something, anything . . .

She climbed out of bed, rummaged in her

backpack, and changed quietly into her cat-burglar costume. It was time for a moonlit game of ultimate sneakage, careful peekage with minimum speakage.

Just as she was about to slip out of the room she heard Oddplop. 'Psst, *amigo*. Hey!' and she looked back over her shoulder.

'You want some company, *amigo*?' shined the little frog. Pippin nodded. In one sec, which is half a second, Oddplop had sprung up onto her shoulder and they'd slipped silently out of the room.

A moment later, they were at the bottom of the stairs and Pippin, by torchlight, was making her way towards the visitors' book. Then something terribad happened. Suddenly, from behind the closed door of the bathroom, Pippin heard somebody flush the toilet! Zoinks! Having to explain to a grown-up why she was dressed like a cat burglar with a bow-tie-wearing frog on her head was not what she needed! Quick as a flash, she leaned her back against one of the corridor walls, pressed her feet on the opposite wall and climbed up, her back wedged on one wall, her legs pressed against the other. As one of the other hotel guests came out of the bathroom in pyjamas and a dressing gown, he passed directly below little Pippin, hiding wedged up high near the ceiling. She watched as the man shuffled along the corridor and went into room number five, locking the door behind him.

Sweet work, amigo, Oddplop Shined to Pippin – the little girl returned the Shine grinning.

Once the coast was clear, Pippin dropped like a silent ninja to the floor. She clicked into search mode and swiftly scanned every page looking for Blowfart's name . . . several times . . .

    🔍 Nothing

    🔍 Nada

    🔍 Nowt

She was
desperately
checking
one final
time for the Doctor's
name when she suddenly saw something
on one of the pages which made her gasp.

Edward Roberts
Babbbins Wood
Funsprings

'Oddplop,' she whispered. 'THIS must be
Blowfart before he became bad! This is my
great-uncle Edward before he lost his special

Shiny friend, Jean the cat, before he set off on the path to being a DARK SHINER!' Supercool Oddplop simply raised one of her froggy eyebrows and nodded gently to show that she had understood.

Buzzing like a bee on its bithday, Pippin read Edward's comments . . .

'Beautiful full moon and a lovely warm welcome from the Boar's Head Hotel. I shall stay again.'

Then Pippin saw something that made her heart beat like a big bass drum. Edward had stayed in room FIVE, the one that dressing-gown guy had just locked behind him.

'I would so LOVE to get a look inside room five,' Pippin whispered to Oddplop, and she tingled with nervous, Shiny energy.

'Close your eyes, *amigo*,' said the little frog, 'and count to three.'

'What are you up to?' asked Pippin.

'Trust me,' replied her little green friend.

Pippin closed her eyes and counted, 'One, two . . .'

In those brief seconds Oddplop sprang off Pippin's shoulder like the world's number one amphibian ninja, bounced like a powerball fired from a cannon into the bar, lifted the spare key to room five, and was back on Pippin's shoulder,

dangling the key and whistling very quietly, by the time the little girl said 'three'.

Grinning, Pippin and Oddplop headed back and there it was: the door to room number five.

Our silent little cat burglar opened the door as quietly as she could and they stepped inside. Pippin looked around the room and saw that the dressing-gown-wearing midnight widdler was now under the covers, snoring like a toothless pig with a clogged-up snout.

Well, at least it's obvious that he's fast asleep, Pippin Shined to Oddplop.

Our hero knew that the chances of finding any sort of clue after this amount of time were about a gazllion to one, and she stood like a statue in the silvery light, thinking about her great-uncle Edward and Jean the cat.

She looked out of the window at the night sky. The full moon was just about to come out from behind a cloud, and Pippin watched, thinking about how it was just the same old moon that had shone on the night Edward had stayed. AND THEN IT HAPPENED – THE AMAZING THING.

The moon came out from behind a cloud

and shone right at the window, which was not a bad aim for the moon considering that it was nearly 240,000 miles away. A single, solitary moonbeam shone into one of the tiny sections of stained glass in the window. This focused the light into a thin red beam, which shot like an arrow across the room and landed on the wall next to the bed.

Pippin crept around the bed, with its snoring inhabitant, and looked at the little red dot of light. Right in the centre, drawn in pencil, was a tiny little X on the wall at the head of the bed.

The little girl's heart raced as she looked at the X. Forgetting that there was actually

111

someone in the bed, Pippin said out loud to Oddplop, 'This was drawn by Edward, I KNOW IT!' From the bed came a grunt and the shadowy figure sat up, still half asleep. Pippin dropped like a sack of potatoes and rolled under the bed, holding her breath as if she was underwater, and waited.

A minute passed and the snoring resumed. As quietly as a fish, Pippin breathed again. She felt instinctively as though she knew what to do. She Shined to Oddplop to help her very quietly check the wooden floorboards under the bed, directly below the X on the wall above.

As they carefully searched around with

their fingertips, suddenly – boom! Maximus floorboardicus – one of them was loose! Pausing for a moment to make sure she could hear snoring once more, Pippin lifted up the loose floorboard and reached into the space. Her eyes widened like saucers as she felt something in the darkness. Then her mouth fell open in disbelief as she pulled out a dusty old leather satchel.

Feeling very nervmouse, she opened the satchel and looked at its contents with a little torch in her mouth. Shiny Pippin pulled out the first thing she could find: it was a map of an island off the coast from Gatacre's Cove.

There were directions and other bits of text on the map. In the torchlight, under the bed in room number five, Pippin's eyes were drawn to the bottom of the page . . .

UNFOLDS SAILS LOOTS

What on earth could that mean? Unfolds Sails Loots? Pippin was frustrated because that made no sense at all, but she knew it had to mean SOMETHING, and also that it could possibly mean EVERYTHING! And so, as silently as a spoon, she rolled out from under the bed and, with the satchel on her back and Oddplop on her head, she crawled out of room number five.

Oddplop fired out her reductable tongue (which is a sciencey term meaning the little frog's tongue was firey-outy and snappy-backy) and looped it around the door handle. As Pippin stood up, Oddplop and her magic tongue very quietly pulled the door closed behind them.

Cheese and
Chutney Sandwich

The next chapter of the story is a little bit difficult for me to explain because it is all about some very mysterious words, and so I am having a Cheshire cheese and chutney sandwich to help me think about how fizzactly to go about telling you – but all I can think is mmmm, jinkies, this IS a delicious Cheshire cheese and chutney sandwich. It is so yummy, it makes me want to sing:

(You know the rules – twenty-five pence.)

I like to eat
Eat, eat, eat
I like to eat
A cheese and chutney sandwich

I like to eat
Eat, eat, eat
I like to eat
A cheese and chutney sandwich

(Reader's voice) *Harry Heape, you are being very frustrating, singing rubbish songs about chutney when you should be telling us what is happening in the STORY!*

You are right. Medium-sized **sozzikins**, I will funtinue . . .

After she had found the dusty satchel in room five, Pippin had decided NOT to go and wake her granny. The little girl knew that they would all need rest before the next part of their **enormous** adventure, and so she and Oddplop had wisely gone back to bed. Clever children know that it is always important to let grown-ups have as much sleep as possible

– it stops them being unpleasant, crotchety and annoying.

Is that the end of the chapter? Because if it is, it was rubbish.

Yes, that is the end of the chapter.

That WAS garbage + rubbish, which WE are going to combine to form a new word – GARRUBBISH. And if you write any more garrubbish chapters, we shall report you to the book police.

I am a lazy pig and I am so sorry for taking you all for grunted. I will make sure the rest of the book is much more betterer.

Soz.

An Excellent Chapter (after the last rubbish one) Called Bananagrams

When Pippin woke the next morning she rolled over and looked towards Mungo's bed.

Her friend was awake but staring sadly into space. It was terrible to see him so down, for as you know from all our earlier adventures, he was usually as jolly as a jumpsuit. Pippin didn't like to see him this way and vowed to get his gold chain back. She so desperately wanted her friend to be able to talk to animals again. When the big man caught Pippin looking at him, he pulled the duvet right over his head. He just wanted to go back to sleep so he could pretend that none of this was really happening.

Pippin rolled over and turned her gaze on her granny's bed. Unlike Mungo, her favourite little old lady was sitting propped up with nineteen pillows, looking as happy as a bum on a toilet. She was very contented because she was eating marshmallows, drinking only the bubbles from a glass of lemonade and doing a crossword puzzle. Granny loved crosswords almost as much as she loved sausage rolls, snooker and sword fighting.

Pippin climbed into bed with the old lady and casually plonked the satchel down beside her. Granny looked at the dusty old bag and her mouth fell open. Then, turning towards Pippin, she peered at her over her respectacles. 'Where in the name of

nine gentleman called Geoffrey did you get that, my dear?'

'Room 5,' replied Pippin. 'I couldn't sleep last night so I went and played a game of cheeky-sneaky-peeky with Oddplop. We found it hidden under one of the floorboards!'

'Oh, you are a clever girl.' Granny gleamed with pride. 'I recognise this bag – it's your great-uncle Edward's!' She was excited about Pippin's discovery but there was also a tinge of sadness in her voice.

'I know,' said Pippin. 'It's got some of his things in it. There's a map and a diary with a lock on it.' She pulled out the map,

unfolding it on the bed. The two of them looked at it for a while.

'Unfolds Sails Loots – what do you think that can mean, Gran? I thought maybe **unfold** the map, **sail** to the island and get the **loot** – maybe it's a treasure map!'

Granny looked at the map and looked down at her crossword. 'It could be a riddle of some sort,' she said, 'or an anagram. If we solve this anagram, it may give us a huge CLUE, which could lead us to the monkeys and dear old Mungo's chain.'

'What's a bananagram, Granny?' Pippin grinned. 'Is it a telegram you send to someone written on the side of a big bendy banana?'

125

'Not exactly,' replied Granny, smiling. 'It's when you take a word or a group of words and rearrange them to make a new word. There are lots of them in crossword puzzles. There's one here, look: the clue is 'LISTEN to no noise' and the answer is SILENT. If you jumble up the letters in 'listen', you can make the word 'silent'.

'Cool,' said Pippin. 'Banagrams should be called funagrams!'

Granny took a notebook out of her bag and she wrote down all the letters that were in UNFOLD SAILS LOOTS so that it looked like this:

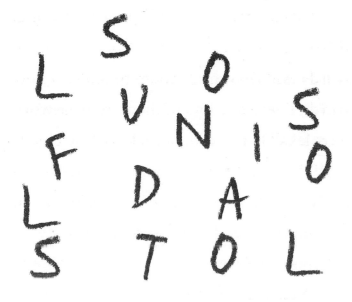

Granny and Pippin stared at the letters for what felt like ages. They each had a couple of marshmallows to help them think. Granny tried making a few new words from the letters on the page. Here is a list of some of the words and phrases that she made.

STALLIONS

TONSILS

A FULL LION

SODA LOTION

'Not really long enough,' muttered Gran thoughtfully, and then, thinking, she wrote another longer one.

UNLOADS LOST FOSSIL

'Unloads Lost Fossil,' said Pippin. 'Haha, that's a good one, Gran! You are as clever as a mushroom!'

'Why, thank you, my dear. I shall take that as a compliment. Mushrooms are known throughout the vegetable world for their huge brainpower.'

Pippin smiled as Granny wrote out another.

A DOLLS FOSSIL SNOUT

'You've got a fossil snout, Gran!' Pippin chimed in, raising her eyebrows.

'You are chirping away like a cheeky chaffinch,' said Gran over her respectactles. 'Why not see if you can help me solve the puzzle?'

'I can make donuts,' said Pippin. 'I could eat a big yummy donut right now,' she added.

Granny smiled. 'You are good at this, my love. Donut is excellent.'

'Haha, Granny, I can make another word which makes me think of you!'

'Ooh, what is it, my dear?' Granny asked. 'I hope it is something lovely, just like donuts.'

'It's TOENAILS,' said Pippin, delighted and collapsing into a fit of giggles. 'Because your enormous toenails are so big that YOU HAVE TO VISIT A BLACKSMITH TO HAVE THEM CUT!'

'You are never allowed to have another one of my marshmallows ever again,' said Granny, and she began to tickle Pippin's alarmpits. 'And you are WRONG by the way, TOENAILS has an E and there is no E in UNFOLDS SAILS LOOTS so you lose a point!'

'Well, I can make Island,' said Pippin. 'So I get two points back for that, and a marshmallow.'

As Granny wrote down Pippin's word, she froze. Gone was the fun that had existed in the room just a second earlier.

'What is it, Gran?' urged Pippin.

'You've got it. We've got it! We've solved it together. You have got the first part and I think I have the second part.' She began to write, and this, my lovely gobblers, is what she jotted down on the page:

ISLAND OF LOST SOULS

It worked. Every letter of UNFOLD SAILS LOOTS was used up.

In that moment, the room became chillier and Pippin cuddled up to her gran. 'Island of Lost Souls,' she said. 'I don't like it. It makes me think of losing Tony again, and it makes me think of ghosts. Maybe that's where the ghost monkeys are from, Gran?'

'Gosh, I think that you could be right,' the little old lady replied. 'The trail always went cold for me at Gatacre's Cove, and thanks to you, I now know why. It's because from here they went out to sea, to this island,' she said, pointing at the map. 'No wonder I could never find them.'

'But now we have a map and we know where we're going – to the Island of Lost Souls!' said Pippin with a shudder.

'We are going on a sea voyage,' said Granny, matter-of-factly.

This was great and very exciting. It was just the sort of thing that could have surfed an enormous wave right out of a wicked adventure story. It was as simple as a pimple, they would go to the island, confront the ghost monkeys and retrieve Mayor Mungo's magical chain. It sounded easy, but there was just one very tiny problem.

Do you know what it was? Any of you? You in the Beauty and the Beast pyjamas, do you know? Yes. That's exactly right, you've nailed it in one.

They did not have a boat.

The Blue Pig

Granny and Pippin knew that there was not a moment to lose and so they quickly began the task of trying to wake Mungo, who had managed to fall back to sleep. Pippin could tell this as, from deep within his duvet, he was making the sort of sound you usually associate with a warthog.

'It's morning and we have a mission,' the old lady and the little girl began to chant loudly, as they speedily packed up their things.

'It's morning time and we have a mission.
It's morning time and we have a mission.
It's morning time and we have a mission!'

Mungo rolled over and peeped out from under the duvet. He opened one eye very slowly, in the way that people do when they are not quite ready to fully wake up, as if having one eye shut means that you are still half asleep. Ha! People are so silly.

'What?' said the big man, slowly opening the other eye.

'It's morning time and we have a mission!' came the reply.

'What mission?' Mungo yawned.

'We need to

137

get a boat,' said Pippin, bouncing. 'Hire a boat, borrow a boat, even steal a boat, but whatever happens this morning, we need a boat,' she insisted. 'The ghost monkeys will be up and away very soon, and we know where they are heading – to the ISLAND OF LOST SOULS! So that's where we are going to get back your chain.'

Mungo jumped out of bed. He could almost feel the magical mayoral chain hanging heavily around his neck again.

'Yes! Find a boat.' The big man was now onside. Smiling at Granny he added, 'Follow the monkeys, retrieve my magical mayoral chain and get back home in time to watch

Antiques Roadshow on your lovely big telly.'

'Fizzactly,' agreed the little old lady with a sparkle, and within moments Mungo, Granny, Pippin and Oddplop were downstairs, with Tony still snoozing and dreaming of hazelnuts in his little friend's pocket.

The morning sunlight poured through the windows of the Boar's Head Hotel. The lovely landlady lady was busy tidying up behind the bar, polishing glasses so that they gleamed and sparkled. 'Good morning, my lovers,' she smiled warmly. 'You look like you're all feeling better after a good night's sleep!'

'Oh, we are, thank you very much,' replied Granny. 'But we are in a flurry of a hurry I'm afraid, and so I would very much like to settle our bill,' she added, taking out a crocodile-skin wallet and handing over a pink fifty-pound bank note.

'I wanted to ask something,' Granny continued. 'We need to hire a boat this very morning and, if possible, someone to sail it for us. We need to visit somewhere called the Island of Lost Souls.'

At the mention of the island, the landlady looked up from what she was doing, gasped loudly, and dropped the glass she was drying. It smashed into a gazillion tiny pieces on the stone floor behind the bar.

'The Island of Lost Souls?' she said after what felt like a chilly eternity. 'I haven't heard anyone mention that place for years. Most say it's just a myth. A made-up place that fishermen talk about after a few too many drinks, to scare each other.'

Our gang looked on at the landlady lady with mouths open. 'Why, there are a thousand scary stories about that place,' the kind lady continued. 'You can't possibly go there, and besides, nobody really knows where it is.'

'What are the stories?' Pippin asked, eager to know everything.

'Well . . .' began the landlady, 'people say that it is shrouded in mist, camouflaged in cloud. It's where dozens of ships and aeroplanes have disappeared and nobody knows why or how. Boats have set off from here in good weather with experienced sea captains and have never returned. They disappear and there's no trace of them. And nobody knows where the island is.'

'We know where it is,' said Pippin.

'We have a map,' added Granny. 'And we can pay a handsome fee,' she smiled, tapping her crocodile-skin wallet, 'to anyone who will hire out a boat and take us there.'

There was another long pause while

the landlady stared past them, before she finally spoke. 'There is only one person in this town who is crazy enough to take you there.'

'Well, who is he?' asked Mungo. 'We need to meet this man immediately.'

'He's not a man, my lover. HE is most certainly a SHE, and she goes by the name of Salty Judith. She's the bravest sea captain between here and Great Rock.'

'So where do we find her?' Mungo asked.

The nice landlady lady looked at them. 'Well, there's a big problem there for you, right away. She's locked up in the police station, down by the harbour. The sergeant was in here last night. He's had to arrest her again.'

'What for?' Granny asked. 'Is she dangerous?'

'No,' replied the landlady lady. 'Well, only to herself, bless her.'

The landlady began to tell them all in hushed tones: 'She was arrested because she had a little bit of fun in here a couple of nights ago. She foolishly bet she could drink a hundred pints of milk. And so, early the next morning, she followed the milkman around town and went to every doorstep after he'd been, and drank the milk that he'd left. She drank nearly four hundred bottles. The sergeant followed a trail of silver milk bottle lids to her home and arrested her.'

Pippin, Granny and Mungo looked at each other, bemused. A minute later, armed with directions to the police station, our intrepid heroes set off with a plan to hire Salty Judith's boat and sail it to the island themselves.

The station was all locked up when they got there and when they knocked on the door, nobody answered. But round the back there was a window with bars, and from it, a very cheesy smell drifted into everybody's nostrils.

Mungo knocked on the bars of the window. 'Salty Judith! Salty Judith! Is that you?'

'Go away,' came the reply. 'I'm not well.'

'We need to ask you a huge favour,' shouted Granny. And Mungo added, 'For money obviously.'

'I don't want money. I feel too icky.'

'I've got a mint which might help you feel a bit better,' shouted Granny. 'I will send my friend in with it.'

Little Oddplop climbed through and delivered a paper bag of Mint Imperials, all the time holding her nose at the smell.

Salty Judith was lying on a bench. She

popped a couple of mints in her mouth and was quiet for a few minutes.

'We would very much like to ask if we could hire your boat.'

'Sure,' said Judith, popping in another couple of mints. 'No problem. Two pound fifty a day.'

'That's very reasonable,' said Granny.

'Going anywhere nice?' asked Judith from deep within the cell.

'The Island of Lost Souls,' shouted Mungo through the bars.

Salty Judith fell off the bench. Then jumping up, she said, 'You're crazier than I am. No one ever comes back from there.

148

No boats come back. No planes come back. Nobody properly even knows where it is!'

'We have a map,' Pippin said temptingly.

Judith appeared at the bars. She had the weathered face of someone who'd spent a lot of time at sea, and dark chocolatey eyes which seemed to hide a hundred secrets. 'I've changed my mind. I am not letting you take my boat,' she said matter-of-factly.

'How about if we pay you to take us there in your boat,' said Granny, studying this curious lady. 'If we can spring you out of jail?'

'Well, then I'd do it for nothing,' Salty

Judith replied with a big toothy grin.

'Stand back,' said Mungo flexing his muscles. 'Time for some Mayor Mungo magic!' The big man grabbed hold of the bars and began to pull as hard as possible, grunting loudly . . . 'Gaaaaaaaaahhhhhhh Grunhhhhffffaaaaaahhhhhhh.'

Then three things happened:

1) He went cross-eyed

2) He went purple

3) He let out a small, hot fart

Meanwhile, Oddplop hopped around the corner, went in through the letter box, lifted the keys from behind the sergeant's desk and released Salty Judith from her cell. Then they both walked out of the police station and round to the back, where Mungo was still straining at the bars like a big sweaty Malcom.

'Looks like you're getting there,' Salty Judith whispered in Mungo's ear. 'Just another good hard pull and I should be free.' She smiled.

'Thanks,' the big man replied.

A moment passed before the penny dropped for the lovely mayor, and he jumped back from the window.

'Gaaah! Weren't you just . . . ?

'How did you . . . ?

'Why wasn't there . . . ?

'Oh never mind! I'm Mungo,' said the big man, his face slowly returning to its normal colour.

'I'm Salty Judith,' grinned their new friend. 'Feared by every coastguard from Land's Ankle to Dawn O'Groats.

'You have sprung me from jail and I am at your command,' she beamed. 'We will do what nobody has managed in a hundred years, we will land on the Island of Lost Souls!'

'There is not a moment to lose,' Pippin added. 'The ghost monkeys may soon be on their way. Take us to your boat.'

'To the *Blue Pig*!' Judith replied, and off they zoomed.

As they ran, with Granny on Mungo's back and the wind in Pippin's hair, our excited little hero felt that everything was possible. Soon she would be whizzing out to sea aboard the *Blue Pig*, destined for adventure on the high seas, in search of the Island of Lost Souls and, most importantly, the stolen mayoral chain.

It wasn't long before they were at the harbour and running along the quay.

They passed boat after boat. There were speedboats and sailing ships and sea-going barges. Salty Judith was ahead, excited to be reunited with the *Blue Pig*. She skidded to a halt next to a huge gleaming white sailboat. The gang caught up and Judith pointed proudly down at the *Blue Pig*.

I am not quite sure how to describe this boat, so I have asked my favourite picture pirate, Rebecca Long-John-Silver Bagley, to draw it for you.

Check it.

Salty Judith beamed with pride, but Pippin could not hide her disappointment at the sight of the *Blue Pig*.

Suddenly, from the other side of the harbour, there came the roar of an engine and the fastest, most futuristic speedboat appeared doing figures of eight in the water – AND IT WAS IN THE SHAPE OF A BANANA.

It sped towards them and there at the wheel were Lumpkin and Bachacha, the ghost monkeys. They waved, raised their hats, and then turned and sped off towards the open sea.

Oh dearie meatballs, my lovers.

Boss-ass Backpack

This was not fair. The ghost monkeys had a boat which looked as though it could have belonged to 007's sister – whose name was was Bond, Dawn Bond – and the heroes of our story had a boat which looked as though it could have belonged to a man called Mr Griffiths who owned a small boating lake in a rubbish park.

THAT however DID NOT MATTER one lovely jot, my friends, because it was not the boat that was important, it was the the people who would be in the boat that really mattered . . .

'I have a splendid idea!' shouted Granny. 'All aboard the *Blue Pig*!' Everyone clambered down a ladder on the quayside. A moment later they were in the little rowing boat and Salty Judith was rowing them very slowly out of the harbour.

Granny pulled out a big bag of useful items that she liked to take on slimportant badventures and began to take things out. First she got out her knitting. 'Nope,' she said, 'not that.' Then she pulled out four bags of marshmallows. 'Mmm. Mallows of Marsh,' she smiled. 'Maybe later . . .' And then finally she pulled out a black backpack. 'Here's my baby,' she said with an enormous twinkle. 'Now we're talking!'

Pippin recognised the backpack immediately from her last terribubble badventure. It was the boss-ass one that had a very powerful jetpack built into it. Granny handed it to Mungo. 'I need you to hold on to this very tightly – it will act as a jet engine for the *Blue Pig*.'

Granny was very clever indeed. With a powerful jet engine on board, they would be able to give those naughty chain thieves a run for their ~~monkey~~ money.

'Hey, Granny!' grinned Pippin, who now looked as happy as a goblin at a farting contest. 'That is a very big and brilliant idea.'

Mungo and Judith sat at the back of the boat and fired up the jetpack. Immediately the boat lurched off at a huge rate of knots, now much more like Dawn Bond's banana speedboat than Mr Griffith's little rowing boat. 'That's better!' Mungo laughed. 'No offence,' he added politely to Salty Judith.

As they zoomed out of the harbour, they spotted a small dot in the distance. It could only be the futuristic vessel of the ghastly ghostly banana twits.

'Follow that boat!' twinkled Granny. Mungo looked down at the dial on the jetpack rucksack. It was at number four. He turned it and they began to gather speed. He turned the speed up gradually – five, six, seven.

Seven felt pretty fast and they hurtled across the water with the wind in their hair and joy in their hearts. I'M FEELING JOLLY EXCITED and I'm not even there! Imagine how they were feeling with seawater spraying up in their faces, chasing a pair of monkey burglars to a magical and dangerous island. Honk-a-doodle-doo, I wish I was a secret special muffin agent sent to do good, and not a book writer sitting in my writing shed in my dungarees with a typewriter on my lap.

Back to the action please.

Pippin shouted over the noise of the jetpack, 'Faster!'

Mungo looked at her, grinned and turned the jetpack up to eight, and then to nine.

This had the effect of making the *Blue Pig* practically supersonic. The little boat now seemed to be speeding along above the water, like a rocket-powered hovercraft. As Pippin and Granny stared ahead, they could clearly see that they were gaining on their thieving foes.

On the banana-bandit boat, Lumpkin and Bachacha knew they were being chased. Bachacha, the slightly bigger monkey who wore the cowboy hat, spoke to his brother. 'Time for some nice little surprises, *mia amico*,' he said.

'I have some surprises, my brother, but they are NOT little and they are NOT nice, hahaha.' And with that he opened a large picnic basket full of plastic bananas and began to hurl them, long and high, in the direction of the *Blue Pig*.

The banana bombs began to rain down all around the *Blue Pig* but there was no way that Salty Judith was going to allow the monkeys of doom to destroy her beloved boat. As they zoomed on in hot pursuit, she dipped her oar in the water on one side and then the other, and the boat veered left, then right, then left again, then right again, and skillfully dodged everything that the monkeys hurled in their direction. The bombs exploded above them, behind them, and all around them, but Judith kept the little supersonic rowing boat safe.

'No more bombs!' said Bachacha on the deck of the banana speedboat. Lumpkin was at the controls in an orange cabin towards the front of the boat. His brother joined him at the wheel. 'Then we outrun them,' Lumpkin said. He pushed the throttle of the boat as far as it would go, and they flew across the waves at the most incredibubble speed.

Our heroes could see that the game had been ratcheted up a few gears and Mungo looked down at the dial on the jetpack. It was on nine. He looked at Judith and then back at the dial. 'Can the *Blue Pig* take any more?' he asked.

'Aye, Captain, she can,' replied Judith confidently, and so the big man moved the dial from nine to ten and then to its fastest setting – ELEVEN.

The *Blue Pig* tore across the waves like a jet plane, skimming the water, getting closer and closer to the banana boat, and before long they were side by side, neck and neck.

Lumpkin and Bachacha were a very cheeky pair of monkeys. They raised their hats and they waved. They danced and they shook their bottoms in the direction of our heroes, and then, worryingly, Bachacha went below deck. He came back a moment later wearing Mungo's precious chain. He danced about with it around his neck and shouted at Mungo, 'Do you like my new necklace, Fishface?'

Mungo turned red with anger. 'That is mine,' he bellowed.

'Finders keepers, losers weepers!' Lumpkin danced and wiggled his bottom in Mungo's direction. This lit Mungo's short fuse and he handed the jetpack to Pippin. 'Judith, get me alongside!' he whispered through gritted teeth.

Judith skillfully steered the boat as close as she could to the monkeys' boat. Mungo stood on the side of the *Blue Pig*, wind in his hair, like a man possessed. The wonderful memory of being able to talk to his animal friends was strong inside the big man's heart. There was no way he was letting that chain out of his sight again.

As the *Blue Pig* came within touching distance of the banana speedboat, Marco joined Roberto at the controls in the orange cabin.

Mungo leaped through the air and landed with a thud on the deck of the rival vessel and he fixed his steely and determined eyes on the two thieves . . . and on his chain. He began to walk towards them, rolling up his sleeves. Then something incredible and unexpected happened, which was unexpected and incredible.

Inside the cabin, Bachacha flicked a switch and out of the top of the cabin came a pair of helicopter blades, which began to turn quickly. Bachacha flicked another button and there was a soft clunk as the cabin detached itself from the rest of the boat.

The chopper blades whirred faster and faster, and as Mungo reached the orange helicopter-chopper cabin, it rose high into the air, leaving the rest of the boat behind. The cheeky monkey pilots raised their hats to Mungo and taunted him by lifting up his

beloved chain, kissing it
and wiggling their bums
to the team below. In a
few moments they were
gone, disappearing into
an area of thick white
cloud that had just appeared,
ominously, on the horizon.

Seventeen
Nice Feelings

I am feeling so disappointy about
how our friends are doing in this
badventure. It feels as though as
soon as they get close to getting the chain
back, they are thwarted.

172

I am sure you are all feeling disappointy too and so I have written a nice poem to cheer us all up. It's about listening to some lovely relaxing music at the same time as eating an enormous cheese and chutney sandwich, and it's called 'Seventeen Nice Feelings'. I hope you like it.

Seventeen Nice Feelings

Seventeen feelings
Seventeen nice feelings
Seventeen nice feelings
In my rum-ti-tum

In my rum-ti-tum-ti-tum

In my rum-ti-tum-ti-tum

In my tum

In my tum

In my tum

In my tum

Ohhhhh

Seventeen feelings

Seventeen nice feelings

Seventeen nice feelings

In my rum-ti-tum-ti-tum

by Harry Heape

Into the Light

ith Mungo back on board but feeling as grumpy as nineteen camels, each with a sore bottom, the team did the only thing that they could do – they set off in the direction of the monkeys' helicopter escape pod.

'Gaah,' said the big man, still fuming.

He was so grumpy that if he had been in a cartoon, steam would have been whistling out of both of his earholes. 'Where DO they get all their cool stuff from? First the banana speedboat, then the banana bombs and now a big escapey helichopter!'

Bright as a button, Shiny Pippin was immediately on the ball. She lifted Edward's satchel onto her lap and pulled out the map to the Island of Lost Souls and showed it to Granny. The little silver-haired old lady looked in the direction of the monkey bandits. 'Full steam ahead, that a-way,' she said, 'while we check the map and work out our exact position.'

Twinkly Granny showed Pippin how to make sure they were going in the right direction. She showed her how to study the skyline and the position of the sun, checking the time on one of her wristwatches. 'Hmm,' Granny said to herself, pulling out a compass from her bag of useful items and looking at the map once more. 'We just keep going due east,' she explained to her little helper.

'Towards that long white cloud,' said Pippin, recalling the words she'd seen earlier on the ancient piece of paper that Granny had carried around with her every day for more than fifty years.

In the land of endless cloud
Lies a mountain that tamed a sun.

'And who knows what we shall find,' said Salty Judith from the back of the *Blue Pig*.

'Bet you a fiver, two poached duck eggs and a belly button full of fluff that we find Blowfart,' replied Mungo.

'I'm calling him Edward from now on,' said Pippin thoughtfully. 'He's not Blowfart any more. We're bringing Edward back. Not Blowfart.'

An almost-tear glistened in the corner of Granny's eye. The old lady wondered how this little girl was becoming so wise.

'Quite right, my dear,' she smiled, squeezing Pippin's hand.

They travelled at speed and with a purpose, and for a little while, with a porpoise. It wasn't long before they were in the thick fog of 'endless cloud'. It really was dense. It was as much as Granny, Mungo and Salty Judith could do to keep the *Blue Pig* pointing due east. They ploughed their way through the fog for more than an hour.

At one point, to try and relieve the boredom of the seemingly endless journey, Mungo blurted out, 'I spy with my little eye, something beginning with F,' and everyone shouted, 'FOG!' He looked sheepish and said, 'All right. Just trying to help pass the time.'

But Granny agreed in principle with Mungo that playing a game would be a good idea to help pass the time.

They played twenty questions, where somebody thinks of a thing and the other people have to ask twenty questions to see if they can work out what the thing is. But nobody could guess the thing that Mungo was thinking about because the thing he was thinking about was one of his uncle's armpits.

Next, Mungo and Pippin had a contest to see how long they could hold their breath. Mungo won this game too, holding his breath for so long that he went as purple as an aubergine and made the fog around his head glow the colour of crimson.

Finally, Mungo suggested a burping game. This involved him burping until Granny got cross and said, 'Enough! Let's play see who can stay quiet the longest.'

They had all been quiet for about five minutes when Pippin spotted something in the distance – a tiny colourful glowing ball of colours, a little bit like the Northern Lights. It shifted between being green and then blue and then orange and then red. It looked mesmerising and magical, and as they approached it got biggerer and biggerer and biggerer.

'I don't like the look of that,' said Granny, as the *Blue Pig* headed through the dense fog. Soon the huge ball of shifting colour ahead of them seemed to be the size of a town.

Was it cloud?

Was it liquid?

Was it some kind of magical gas ball?

It was like nothing that they had ever seen in their lives. And they were heading straight for it.

Q) Was it dangerous?

A) Oh dreary me – maybe.

Perhaps it was the thing that had destroyed all of the ships and aeroplanes that the landlady had talked about? Perhaps they might all be about to be vapourised or plucked from the sea and transported to another dimension. It was all very scary indeed.

Pippin suddenly felt as though the most important thing in the world at that moment was to hold hands, and she reached out to Granny and the others. She remembered the first terribubble badventure with Granny, when they had been on Oswald the stag's back, close and TOGETHER. At the end of her last badventure, they had all held hands at the top of the scary lighthouse, Timon Keep.

The little girl was exactly the same amount of frightened as they headed towards the alien light. She wanted to feel a hand in hers and she also *knew* that they were stronger as a group than each of them were individually.

'Everyone, keep holding hands!' the little girl cried out as they flew towards the strangeness.

The power was too much. Mungo turned off the jetpack and pulled everyone in to a protective cuddle. 'EVERYONE, CLOSE YOUR EYES!' said Granny fiercely, and they shut their eyes tightly, not knowing whether they would survive crashing into this strange and colourful intergalactic light show.

As they passed through into the light bubble there was the most incredible sound. It was as though a thousand sirens, foghorns and sailors' screams were ringing in their ears and coursing through their souls. An echo of the fear and panic of all the people who'd perished trying to find the island.

And then all at once there was total calm, and a deep warmth spread across the faces of our heroes. 'Don't open your eyes,' Granny urged again. 'We are not out of danger yet. Keep them closed, whatever you do!' The boat drifted and drifted, and our heroes all held on to each other with their eyes tightly shut.

They heard the grinding crunch of sand and stone beneath the boat and the *Blue Pig* suddenly stopped.

They waited for several minutes. All of them quiet. All of them scared until Granny spoke. 'Okay,' she said. 'Very slowly. Everybody, open your eyes.' They did, and looked around them. The cold,grey ocean and dismal fog had gone. Instead they saw the most incredibubbley beautiful landscape that any of them could have possibly ever imagined, even in their very wildest dreams.

They had landed on a beautiful white sandy sun-drenched beach, dotted with palm trees. Astonishingly colourful birds with huge wingspans glided silently around in the sky. The beach led up to dense jungle out of which reared enormous rocky outcrops. The jungle stretched as far as the eye could see. In several places, there seemed to be clearings around the most gigantic rocky cliffs, with waterfalls and pools which looked inviting and wonderful.

At the very centre of the island was an enormous volcano, so tall that it kissed one or two clouds high in the brilliant bright blue sky.

Pippin whispered to herself, '*In the land of endless cloud, lies a mountain that tamed a sun*'.

Perched on the side of the volcano was a temple. It looked huge, even from down on the beach. It was white marble with several red-domed roofs and towers, and its shiny windows twinkled and sparkled in the tropical sunlight.

Everyone stood and stared. None of them

had ever seen anything quite like this before. 'Right,' said Granny, and she pulled up her tights and adjusted her thunderpants. 'Well, isn't this nice?' she added with a smile, 'I suppose we'd better make a plan'. They had only been on the island for a few minutes but what they didn't know was that, from the edge of the forest, they were already being watched by a pair of very beady eyes. Very, very beady indeed.

Two Locks
and One Key

It's time, my lovely friends, for me to tell you what was happening with the bad guy of our story – Doctor Blowfart. Here is a picture from the world's number one picture wizard, Chewbacca Wiggley, to help us remember just how much of a rotten gas valve he really is.

Blowfart was not far away from our lovely heroes. He was in his workshop in the marble temple on the side of the volcano. The workshop was set up like a blacksmith's forge with bright orange glowing fires, and anvils and hammers and stands and leather aprons, and all kinds of other bits of very blacksmithy stuff.

The Doctor was at work, no doubt forging an evil plan. His face was lit by orange light as he concentrated on making the fires glow hot with hatred. Gareth, his mean white cat, sat curled on a cushion on a shelf above him, enjoying the hideous warmth.

Suddenly there was a timid knock at the door. 'Enter,' said Blowfart, not even looking up from what he was doing. Now then, my favourite book-gobbling friendly friends, can you guess who was about to come through that door?

Q) Was it the Queen of
Denmark?

A) No

Q) Was it Daphne and Velma
from *Scooby Doo*?

A) No

Q) Was it Scooby himself?

A) No. Look, you're way off, so
I'm going to have to tell you.

It was the terrible monkey burglars,
Lumpkin and Bachacha! THAT'S who.

'Well,' whispered Blowfart menacingly.
'Do you have it?'

'Yes, my Lord,' said Roberto, taking off

his cowboy hat and acting like a naughty schoolboy entering the study of a mean old headmaster.

'Bring,' said the spindly Doctor, still not even looking up from his work. Lumpkin and Bachacha, hats in hand, approached cautiously and laid Mungo's mayoral chain on the workbench next to where Blowfart was working.

'You have served me well,' slithered the sinister smith. 'Now be gone,' he said, and the monkeys crept out as quickly as they could.

The dark and Shiny Doctor took the chain and lifted a pair of heavy blackened bolt cutters from the shelf. Very carefully, he snipped off a couple of sections of the golden chain. Gareth jumped silently down from his comfy cushion onto the workbench and began to strut.

'Do you know what I am about to do, Gareth?'

'No, sir,' purred the cat. 'I don't. But whatever it is, I'm sure it will be deliciously rotten and frightfully unkind,' he added with a mean miaow.

'You know me well,' answered Blowfart, 'but that is not quite right. What I am going to do is not rotten and unkind – YET. What I actually have planned right now is fantastically shrewd, slick and very skilful.'

Gareth listened as the Doctor explained. 'I am going to take a little bit of this magical gold, gold rich in Shiny alchemy that came from the mines beneath Funsprings. And I am going to melt it down and then pour it into a mould to make a magical golden key, my precious one.'

'Delicious,' purred Gareth the cat.

'My mother's prophecy is clear to me now, Gareth: *A lock which cannot be undone by a simple key for the upstairs.* My key is not simple – it is very special as it is made from a Shiny magical gold. I am going to turn it inside a lock upstairs and then . . . then, when the clock strikes midnight, I will complete the mission described in the note left to my mother.'

Blowfart looked down at Gareth and grinned an evil grin. 'And then,' the evil Doctor began, 'we will see who will become the most dangerous Shiner of their generation.'

Hahahahaha hahahahahahaha hahaha

Long Thin Sofas

Down on the beach, the heroes of this story were looking up at the temple on the side of the volcano. They had no idea of the unpleasantness that you and I have just witnessed, my adorable little chocolate-chip book dumplings.

Granny and Pippin were trying to work out how to get from the beach to the beautiful white marble building perched proudly high above them. 'There is only one thing stopping us,' said Pippin, scratching her brown curls.

'I know,' replied Granny. 'The enormous impenetrable jungle, which is probably full of scarrifying snakes and granny-eating tigers.'

'Gaaaah,' said Mungo. 'I am not setting foot anywhere where there might be snakes or tigers. They scare my beak off. I would rather fight nineteen sharks in a bathtub than even look at a picture of a tiger, and don't talk to me about snakes – I hate them, they're so snakey and wiggly and bad.'

Pippin calmed Mungo down by saying things like 'there, there' and 'don't worry'. Granny explained that snakes would be more scared of an enormous Mungo crashing through the jungle and that they would slither off into their homes and hide behind their long thin sofas.

Luckily Mungo calmed down. Looking back at the jungle, Pippin and Granny were stumped. Neither of them had ever had to trek through a jungle before and they were both feeling a little bit worried

about getting lost. The same thought crossed both their minds at the same time and they exchanged glances – it would be *very easy* to get badly lost in there.

Oddplop was sitting on a rock trying not to get sand on her little green froggy bottom. She saw Edward's diary poking out of Granny's bag of useful items and she dragged it onto the sand and hopped on top of it. It was an old leather book with a brass lock.

While Granny and Pippin were pacing

and contemplating the dangers of the jungle, Oddplop hopped up onto the little old lady's shoulder and whispered, 'Excuse me, I just want to borrow one of your hairgrips.' She carefully removed a hairgrip from Granny's hair, and in a second she'd sprung silently back down onto the leather diary and had begun to try and pick the lock of the ancient book. In a moment, the lock flicked open.

'Ahem. *Amigos*. Hey!' she shouted in her tiny green voice. Granny and Pippin looked down as Oddplop pointed at the book. It had blown open, and right in the middle pages was a map of how to get from the beach to the temple.

'Oh, Oddplop,' said Granny, 'you are indeed a gifted and very smart tiny lady.'

This made Oddplop feel as nice as a nest. She blushed and dusted little bits of invisible dirt off her little shoulders and blew her fingernails very gently.

Windy

I

am

trying   to

write   this

chapter   outside

                          k

in   the   par

but   it

is   **VERY**

    w   i   n

d   y

and   all

my

          words   have

                              WHERE

     Blown   EVERY

Oh

heck

.

Harry

Heape

xxxxxxx

16

Wiggly Vicky

The beady eyes were still watching our nice people very carefully. It was not very often that humans made it to this island and the creature watching them was feeling very nervmouse. It is often not good when an animal is nervous. That can be when they are at their most dangerous.

(Reader's voice) *Tell us what the animal was please, Harry. Was it a lion?*

No, it wasn't a lion or a leotard – I MEAN LEOPARD! Nor was it a cheetah or jaguar. You will need to read on because you'll get no spoily-spoilers from me.

Unaware of the spying eyes, Granny, Pippin, Mungo and Salty Judith gathered up their things, while Tony snoozed quietly in Pippin's pocket. He was having the most lovely dream about being the mouse king at a special pecan-and-pistachio themed feast given in his honour.

Oddplop sat on top of Mungo's lovely big noggin, looking towards the trees.

'Hey, *amigos*,' she called suddenly. The little frog had spotted something orange at the edge of the jungle and they rushed over to investigate. There, partially hidden behind an enormous rock, was Lumpkin and Bachacha's escape helicopter and IT STILL HAD THE KEYS IN IT!

'Maximum treasure!' grinned Mungo. 'Let's fly this bad boy up to the temple,' he added. 'I'm probably wicked at flying helicopters,' he said, looking up at the temple and back at the helicopter. Granny studied him over the top of her respectacles, very much objecting to his use of the word 'probably'.

'That would be way too noisy,' said Judith. 'You might as well ring the monkeys and tell them you're on your way.'

'Quite right,' agreed Granny. 'Whatever's going on up there, I want us to arrive more quietly than the fart of a librarian. I think we'll stick with the map that Oddplop found,' she decided.

Twinkling like a sugary donut, Pippin suddenly had a very high-quality idea. 'Hey, Judith, why don't you stay here with the chopper,' suggested the little girl, grabbing a walkie-talkie from Granny's bag. 'You can act as backup – if we need rescuing we'll call and you can fly us to safety.'

'That is a deal,' grinned Salty Judith. 'An ideal deal,' she added, climbing into the helicopter. Judith reclined one of the seats and turned on the radio, which was playing some very relaxing reggae. 'I'll snooze here in the sunshine – I MEAN STAY HERE AND BE VERY ALERT. Get in touch if you need me.'

Our team were now ready for their very dangerous journey. Oddplop sprang onto Pippin's head and Granny climbed up onto Mungo's broad back for a piggyback ride. This was no problem for the big man because he was as strong as five angry toilets and Granny was very light because, as you well know, she only ate marshmallows and Monster Munch, and she only ever drank the bubbles from lemonade.

The mystery creature with the spying eyes had decided to investigate our team a little closer and was sneaking towards them high up in the treetops above where they walked.

Granny, from her lofty perch, was in charge of map-reading. 'We are on a path which I am pretty sure is this path *here*,' she said, pointing at the map inside Edward's diary.

'Yay, I love maps!' said Mungo. 'You

know where you are with a map! Do you get it? You know . . . where you are . . . with a map!'

As Mungo mucked about like a goat at a chicken party, high up above them the mystery animal was getting closer, and closer, and closer, and the heroes of our story did not have the slightest idea.

'Your jokes will be hugely important on this journey,' Granny said, smiling at Mungo. 'They will keep our spirits up.'

'I AGREE,' Pippin agreed. 'They will make the time fly by as quickly as a shmickly pickly, and before you know it, we shall have your chain and be heading home in a stolen helicopter to gobble mallows of marsh on a comfy sofa.'

It was at that moment that the mysterious animal chose to crash their lovely scene.

Booom!

Hiss! 'Hello!'

A GIANT SNAKE UNFURLED ITSELF FROM A BRANCH ABOVE AND DANGLED IN FRONT OF MUNGO SO THAT HE CAME FACE TO FACE WITH THE ENORMOUS SLITHERY MONSTER.

'Gaaaaaaaaaah,' the big man screamed and fainted. Just before he hit the ground, Granny jumped off and did a forehead roll, which is very much like a forward roll but a little more 'ouch, my head'.

Granny leaped up and stood next to Pippin, guarding the little girl as they watched the huge snake dangling in front of them while Mungo regained consciousness. The big man rubbed his head, shuffled backwards on his bottom and hid behind the little girl and the even littler old lady.

To their great surprise the snake spoke to them in an extremely friendly voice. 'Well, *he's* a big sssscaredy bottom isn't he?'

'He's just not sure about snakes, that's all,' Pippin answered, protectively.

Mungo was surprised to be able to understand the snake – it was because of the incredible Shiny magic of the Island of Lost Souls. That magic here was so strong, EVERYBODY and EVERY ANIMAL was Shiny.

'You don't need to worry about me,' said the snake. 'I'm your new chum. My name's Wiggly Vicky.' Mungo shuffled on his bottom a little bit closer to the others. 'You must be heading up to the volcano,' hissed Vicky. 'That's where all the animals who look like you go. I can sssshow you the quickessst way, if you like?'

Granny and Pippin scratched their heads and looked at the huge snake. Could she be trusted? Or was this a trap?

Wiggly Vicky the snake, seemingly oblivious, dropped from the tree and began to slither along the path, chatting nonsense to herself as she went. 'I'm nine years old and I love to slither and wiggle,' she babbled. 'Slithering and wiggling on sand is my favourite and best because you can make lovely patterns with your underbelly and it is very tickly.'

'As tickly as a feather in your armpit?' asked Pippin, jogging to catch up with this funny creature.

'I know what a feather is but I have never even heard of an armpit,' said Wiggly Vicky. 'IT SOUNDS VERY TICKLY!'

'Oh, it is,' smiled Pippin, whose armpit suddenly felt tickly even at the mention of a feather. 'Armpits are very tickly indeed,' she smiled.

Granny and Pippin beamed at each other. This snake was not snakey. In fact, this snake seemed like the most unsnakey snake in the history of snakes.

'I saw you on the beach when I was

going for my morning wiggle,' Wiggly Vicky continued. 'I go there three times a day – for a morning wiggle, an afternoon wiggle and a wiggle before bedtime. Wiggling's the best. Do any of you wiggle?'

Pippin hung back and whispered to Granny and Mungo, 'This snake seems adorable. I think she's nice.'

'Thanks!' said Vicky, who had not been meant to hear that bit. 'I have great hearing for someone who looks like they have no ears!'

'You sure do,' shouted Pippin.

'I'd be in real trouble if I ever needed glasses though!'

Pippin laughed and smiled at Granny.

'I can't believe we are following a snake called Vicky that's got banter,' said Mungo, who was now feeling slightly less scared.

Vicky continued her nice hissy chatter. 'There's a ssssecret passageway that leadsss right up through the fiery mountain. I'll slither on my nice soft tummy and take you there.'

This made Granny smile and she put the map back in her pocket. 'It will take hours and hours off your journey,' the snake added. 'There's only one tiny wiggly problem. The secret passage is guarded by the second biggest tiger in the world.'

Gasp-a-doodle-doo, book goons! This terribubble badventure was certainly not becoming any easier for poor Pippin and her intrepid friends.

I am not enjoying this particular section of the book and I don't mind telling you that I wouldn't fancy swapping places with our heroes at this moment in time, not for all the chutney in Chester.

Edward's Diary

The path through the jungle opened up a little and they came to a small clearing with a rock to sit on. Very conveniently the rock was exactly the right size for the bottoms of all of our heroes, so they sat and drank tea from a flask, which Granny magically produced as if from nowhere. Pippin watched as Mungo got up and began to pace up and down. She could see that he was trying to gear himself up for coming face to face with the world's second biggest tiger.

Granny fished Edward's diary out of her bag and she and Pippin began to leaf through it. It fell open at a page which had been marked with a photo of Edward and his beloved cat Jean. Granny and Pippin shared a very sad glance as they both began to read the page.

I have it on the next page, just as it was written by Edward, all those years ago.

Dear Mother,

I have come to the end of the worst day of my life. I am writing what happened today in the hope that I can one day make some sense out of it.

Jean and I have made it to the island in your prophecy and so much is clear to me now about the words that appeared on your bedside all those years ago.

I write to you from the land of the endless cloud. This is the island fishermen call the Island of Lost Souls. There is magic here that is beyond anything that we have dreamed about. It's a place where all animals are Shiny.

My sister and I are so lucky we have Oswald and Jean. We have the power of Shining and it is the most wonderful gift, but here on the island there is the magic of nine galaxies. I have pieced together clues and this is what I believe: the night the star exploded in Funsprings and gave us our Shiny powers, it was followed by a much larger, more magical star.

As it hurtled to Earth, the large star separated from the smaller star and landed in Funsprings. The bigger star did not want to damage our beautiful planet and so it crashed into the crater of a volcano. I believe that the volcano was <u>the mountain which</u>

tamed the sun. I think the sun in your prophecy was this huge, very magical star.

This star had the power of nine magical galaxies and it buried itself in the mountain. Magic poured into the island. Many of its animals became shiny and kind and wise and good.

The island began to think for itself. I think that it knew that it had to keep itself hidden, so it surrounded itself with fog and an ingenious electrical magnetic light which baffled sailors and sent them off course. Everyone who looked directly at the centre of the light was steered away from the area.

I only survived through luck, as my instinct was

not to look at it at all costs, I don't know why. And so I found myself here, and now wish more than anything that I had stayed away, for something truly terrible happened before I could unravel the second part of the note that was left on your bedside, Mother In the upstairs of the temple, in the highest room, there is a door with a door which, as you predicted, cannot be undone with a simple key. I have tried for months with Jean but no luck.

One afternoon, exasperated by our lack of success, we were walking on the rim of the crater of the volcano. We had a picnic and were playing, jumping from rock to rock. It was a relief to be away from that door. And then it happened. I can hardly bring myself to tell you that I was showing off on the edge of the crater, like a fool, trying to make Jean laugh. She told me to step away from the edge but I lost my footing and fell backwards into the volcano. Jean sprang but she was too late, she couldn't stop me falling. I was heading for a sticky end, and then the magic happened. Something on this magical island helped me. The animals are all so kind and wise here, and Jean, in a heartbeat, swapped her life for mine.

She gave me her life. In a second I was sitting back on the edge of the volcano and Jean had disappeared forever. I never saw what happened to her. I looked and looked all day and all night and all the next day, but she's gone and I am distraught.

I cannot come home. I will stay and search for Jean but I feel an emptiness inside as though I know that she is truly gone. I am so sorry for what I have done.

Edward X

By the time they came to the end of the page, Granny and the little girl were in floods of tears.

'Oh, dearest Pippin. My poor brother. I can see why he blames himself but this was an accident. That's clearer to me than ever. Who in their life has never slipped and fallen? It's just that Edward slipped and fell at the worst possible moment . . .' She tailed off.

'And Jean saved him,' said Pippin, staring at the letter. 'No wonder he's never forgiven himself. That's why he keeps coming back to life, Gran,' said Pippin. 'Jean gave him her nine lives.'

'My dear, clever girl, you have it,' whispered Granny. 'The mystery of how he keeps returning. HE HAS NINE LIVES – just like a cat!'

'He doesn't have nine any more,' said

Pippin, as sharp as a tack.

'You're right,' said Granny, counting them on her little fingers. 'He lost one at the volcano, which means eight.'

'He lost one in a battle with Oswald and me many years ago,' she added, 'when we thought that he was gone for good.'

'That makes seven,' said Pippin, 'and he lost one with with me above the mines, which makes six, AND one at the top of Timon Keep – FIVE!'

'So we know he has five lives left,' Granny said at last. 'That means we have five chances to bring him back to good.'

This felt like a big DISCOVERY.

They now knew that Blowfart couldn't just keep coming back over and over. They had to put a stop to this. Granny knew deep in her bones that she would find him up in the temple, and after reading that letter, it seemed more important than ever to bring back the old Edward. So, filled with an icy determination, Granny called Mungo, who had wandered off to throw stones at a tree to try and take his mind off enormous tigers.

Ingrid the Tiger
Is Not a Giraffe

Back on track in the jungle, Granny and Pippin had wiped away their tears and were focusing on getting Edward back. Wiggly Vicky slithered along on the path ahead of them, still wittering on to herself. 'My mother was a snake, you know, and my mother's mother before her. You could say I come from a long line of snakes! A long wiggly line!' Vicky continued. 'My mother used to get quite upset that everybody was scared of snakes because we are actually very friendly. As a species, we're quite misunderstood.'

Up ahead, Wiggly Vicky stopped and raised herself up. She nodded along the path and the others stopped and looked. Ahead of them they could see that the path opened up into a very large clearing, which ended at a craggy cliff face. Down the front of the cliff face tumbled a huge and very beautiful waterfall, behind which was a cave with a narrow entrance. Sitting on the grass in front of the waterfall was the second largest tiger in the world. She was huge, the size of a small car. She was fast asleep and her snoring was a mixture of a purr and a deep rumbling roar. It was so deep that as she snored, the leaves of the nearby trees shook and rained down as if it was autumn.

The gang approached cautiously, with Mungo hanging back, feeling nine hundred per cent nervous about the tiger. They paused a safe distance away and studied their options.

'We could just try and sneak past?' suggested Pippin.

'Na-na-na-na-na,' interrupted Mungo. 'Knowing my luck, I would tread on a twig and then bingo, it would be time for the tiger who came to tea – if you know what I mean.'

'I could distract the tiger,' suggested Pippin, 'then run huge circles around the jungle and come back when the tiger is dizzy and meet you inside?'

'Too risky – tigers are quick,' replied Granny.

'Look,' said Oddplop from the top of Granny's head. On the cliff, to the side of the waterfall, was a sign. Everybody peered. The little frog was right. The sign

was just too far away to read so Granny
pulled out her binoculars and had a look.

Granny read out the words on the poster.
'Oh no!' groaned Mungo. 'This is really bad!

INgRid the tigeR
IS NoT A giraffe
Guards This dooR
'Til you Make her
laugh
You have tHree chances
to pick a winneR
Make Ingrid laugh or ...
be her DinneR

There's nobody funnier than me *usually* but the last couple of days have really knocked my confidence.'

Granny and Pippin looked downcast. When he was his normal self, Mungo would have been just the man to make people laugh. The big man saw the disappointment written on their faces. 'I suppose I could give it a try. Maybe the pressure will help me perform.'

'Are you sure you're okay to risk it?' asked Granny. 'You won't be too afraid?'

'No! A comic lives on his wits,' replied Mungo bravely. 'Fear will give me the edge!'

Meanwhile, Tony had climbed up onto

Pippin's shoulder and was whispering to her. They decided what they needed was a little backup plan that would help the big man if his jokes did not do the trick.

Tony whispered a final something into Pippin's earhole, and with that, she and Tony began to climb a nearby tree. Mungo paced back and forth, searching for a joke, even just a small one . . . 'I've got it at last!' he said. 'I shall do tiger jokes. Perfect.'

With an uneasy feeling in her old bones, Granny went towards the tiger. 'Excuse me, Ingrid.' The tiger opened one eye. She did not look pleased to be woken up. 'I'm sorry to wake you,' Granny continued, 'but we should like to pass through the waterfall. My friend has a joke that we hope you will enjoy.'

Mungo shuffled towards the enormous tiger, taking tiny cautious steps and playing with his sleeves, and then he delivered his killer joke:

'Why did the tiger . . . lose at poker?'

Ingrid did not look impressed and waited for the punchline.

'Because he was playing with a cheetah!'

Mungo grinned sheepishly and bowed.

Some tumbleweed blew across the clearing and Mungo's words were met with something that was more silent than absolute silence. The tiger uncurled one of her huge claws. Scratching, she drew a mark on the cliff wall and then spoke.

'The oldest joke in the world,' she said. 'That joke has never EVER been funny. Strike one.'

Mungo gulped, and the tiger stood up, brushing a big pile of bones to one side and beginning to patrol the cave entrance.

Meanwhile, on a branch high above the clearing, Pippin and Tony were plotting and planning and whispering. Tony began to nibble on a vine which hung from the tree.

Down below, Mungo cleared his throat and began to speak. His voice, noticeably thinner and reedier than before:

'Why don't tigers . . . eat clowns?'

'Because they taste funny,' growled Ingrid. 'The second oldest joke in the world. That one WAS funny the first time it was told MORE THAN TEN THOUSAND YEARS AGO!' The enormous tiger drew another mark on the wall next to the first one. 'Strike two. Nearly yummy idiot o'clock.'

Mungo was really frightened, but instead of thinking carefully about what to do next, he rushed into his last joke.

'What . . . what . . . what did the tiger say to her cubs?'

'Oh no,' said Pippin. She could see the tiger begin to uncurl all her claws. She had to help Mungo – the time was NOW – so she jumped onto a vine hanging from the highest branch and swung down like Tarzan, hurtling through the air, the wind whistling in her hair, heading straight towards her friend who was about to deliver the punchline to the third worst joke in the world. She was a split second away. Before she lifted Tony the mouse up out of her pocket, she heard Mungo delivering his punchline:

'Don't cross the road until you see the zebra cro—'

But before he could finish the final word of the joke, Pippin whizzed past him and stuffed Tony head first into Mungo's mouth like a cork into a wine bottle. The big man was silenced. All you could see was Tony's chubby bottom and tail wiggling around.

The tiger looked on in amazement. Flying through the air had been so exciting

248

for the little mouse that he let out a long high-pitched hazelnutty mouse fart. The watching Tiger had never seen anything so funny in his life and roared with joy.

Roaarrrrrahhahahahhaha! Ooooohahahahaha! Ahahaha-hahahaha!

She rolled on the floor, she beat the ground with her enormous paws and when she finally stopped laughing she looked up with tears in her eyes.

'I've never laughed so much in all my life. The passageway. Hahahaha. Be my guests. Off you go. Knock yourselves out hahahahaha . . .'

With that little section of the mission now completed, our team said goodbye to Wiggly Vicky and walked into the cave. They were expecting a slow and difficult climb up through the mountain, maybe up an ancient stone staircase with booby traps and a zombie army, but what they saw surprised them all. Inside was a golden lift. The doors opened and they stepped in. They looked at the buttons and pressed the one at the very top.

The lift juddered and began to take them to their final destination.

No Chance, Harry

Oh no. This is another one of those chapters that I am not fancying, thank you very much for asking. Too scary. I've tried to get my good friend Rebecca Von Wiggley to draw us a few nice pictures at the beginning of this chapter. I asked for some baby owls in a nest and some little guinea pigs wearing bandanas, that sort of thing, but she told me, 'No chance, Harry. You know what you have to do. You've got to tell them what happened. Even if it's bad.'

She's right. Gulp. Here goes.

So, as the lift was making its way slowly up through the mountain, Blowfart, wearing Mungo's magical chain, was excitedly making his way to his blacksmith's forge again.

'Now, Gareth,' began the evil Doctor, 'the time has come to fulfil the prophecy!' and he began to recite it.

'In the land of endless cloud
Lies a mountain that tamed a sun
With the power of nine galaxies
And a lock which cannot
    be undone
By a simple key for the upstairs-
upstairs you will need
Golden drops one, two, three
For two of the gifted there must be
Through four gateways
    tread carefully
To Everywhere, Adventure
    & Eternity
And one more to bring you home

'We have the key, Gareth! You and I are Shiners, so we are two of the gifted. Upstairs we will go, to every adventure and eternity. Now. THE KEY.

Hahahahaha hahahahahahaha hahaha

Blowfart scuttled along like a bad beetle, wringing his hands and dreaming of world domination. Gareth strolled behind him, chest puffed up like a big, silly playground bully.

In a moment they were both in the forge. Blowfart lifted the mould which contained the key that he had made earlier from a couple of the links from Mungo's magical chain.

'Let's hope this has now cooled, Gareth,' said Blowfart, licking his small, thin, chickeny lips. He turned the mould over and tapped it with a small metal hammer. The key fell out and jangled satisfyingly on the metal table below.

'Excellent,' said Blowfart, which is a word that baddies just love to use over and over again. He popped the key into his pocket. 'Upstairs,' he said quietly.

Blowfart and Gareth exited the forge and turned right along a marble corridor, coming to a stop outside a lift. The evil Doctor pressed the button to call the lift and waited. A few moments later, guess what happened – the doors opened.

Honk-a-doodle-doo and nine hundred and forty-five jinkies. What unlucky timing!

Inside the lift was the good team – Granny, Pippin and Mungo! Oddplop was perched on Granny's shoulder. Tony, as usual, was snoozing in Pippin's pocket.

Our friends were so astonished to see the Doctor right there in front of them,

they were all completely speechless. The Doctor, however, didn't seem surprised at all, for his mind was on FAR BIGGER THINGS. He stepped into the lift and pressed the button to take them to the top floor of the temple.

'Excellent!' he said again, turning towards his enemies. 'I've been expecting you, although I really thought you'd be here sooner. I hear my ghost monkeys gave you the slip a couple of times.' His eyes narrowed and without Pippin or Granny realising it he Shined a very dark, secret telepathic Shine made up of just three words: *Lumpkin, Bachacha. Visitors.*

'Edward, listen, we have come to help you,' said Granny.

'It's time for you to come home,' added Pippin, looking at the Doctor with big brown eyes.

'My name is Blowfart!' bellowed the Doctor. 'And there is NO coming home. I live here now.'

As soon as he had spoken those words, the lift came to a stop. The doors opened and the team could see they were at the top of the temple, on a balcony overlooking the island at the building's very highest point. At one end of the balcony was a door with a very ornate golden keyhole.

In a puff of smoke, the ghost monkeys appeared, as if from nowhere. In an instant, they whizzed around our team and tied them up tightly with rope. Blowfart clicked his fingers, and as quickly as they'd arrived, the monkey burglars left in a puff of very farty banana mist.

Blowfart paced. 'Mother's prophecy. The power of nine galaxies. It shall be mine!

Hahahahaha hahahahahahaha hahaha

'Come back with us, Edward,' said Granny.

'We know what happened with Jean,' added Pippin. 'You lost her in a terrible accident and she gave you her nine lives. It was a really horrible thing that could have happened to anyone. It wasn't anyone's fault.'

'IT WAS MY FAULT,' bawled the Doctor. 'Jean is gone forever.'

'You don't know she's gone forever,' Pippin urged. 'There is magic way bigger at work here. You know that. Maybe Jean gave you eight lives? Maybe she survived the fall. Maybe she's somewhere waiting to be found!'

Blowfart looked at the little girl. This seemed to be something he had not even considered. For a moment a flicker of hope crossed the old man's face. He looked tired and, taking off the heavy chain, put it down on a small table. Out of the Doctor's line of vision, Pippin Shined to Tony, *Nibble the rope. Imagine it is an enormous yummy hazelnut.*

Tony the mouse opened his eyes, snuck out of Pippin's pocket and used his little razor-sharp teeth to start gnawing through the rope.

The Doctor was deep in thought. 'Jean is gone. I searched for years. Time to get over it!' And with that, he pulled the key out of his pocket and went over to the door.

What would happen when he opened that door? There was no telling. It could be disastrous. Tony was almost through the thick rope. Were our team too late to stop Blowfart from channelling a limitless amount of Shiny magic? This would be bad news. He would be unstoppable.

The
Upstairs-Upstairs

Up on the balcony, Blowfart walked slowly towards the door with Gareth slinking smugly behind him. The Doctor slowly took the key out of his pocket and held it carefully in his trembling hand.

'Don't do it!' said Granny. 'I have a bad feeling about that door. This magic is ever so powerful and we know very little about it! Edward, it could be the end of us all if you open that door.'

'Nonsense! And my name is NOT Edward,' snapped Blowfart. 'You also forget that if I die, I shall just come back again.'

The truth was that Blowfart did not know where this door would lead. He was obsessed by the prophecy, convinced he was heading towards Everywhere, Adventure and Eternity, places that would give him even more Shiny powers and, he hoped, untold riches and opportunity for naughtiness.

The Doctor put the key in the door and slowly began to turn it. At that moment Tony nibbled through the rope and it fell to the ground. Blowfart looked over his shoulder at them. 'Too late, my rubbish friends. Hahahahaha. I'm about to pass through the magical door of the prophecy!'

The old man turned the key and leaned into the door. Nothing. The magical key wasn't working! He tried again and again. Nothing. Blowfart began to fume.

'This is your fault!' he screamed directly at Pippin. 'You have been nothing but trouble and YOU ARE STOPPING ME

FROM CONCENTRATING. It's time to finish you for good!' And with evil intent in his eyes, he began to stride towards our hero, rolling up the sleeves of his labcoat.

Mungo could not stand by and risk his beloved friend Pippin getting hurt! He reached for the nearest thing he could find – the magical mayoral chain.

'Begone!' he bellowed, and flung it at Blowfart as hard as he possibly could. As it flew through the air, it seemed to Shine and glow with tremendous magical energy.

The chain caught the Doctor right on the end of his long and unpleasant conk, and it did something which was both funexpected and incredibubble. The chain passed through the Doctor as if he were made of air and crashed into the wall behind him right next to the door.

Blowfart let out an anguished scream. The Shiny magic gold had released its ancient, kind power upon the horrid, mean Doctor. Then, just as he had done in the forest around Funsprings and at the top of the lighthouse at the end of their last terribubble badventure, Blowfart exploded into a huge cloud of shimmering ancient sparkles of starlight.

As the shimmering, glistening particles rained down on the marble floor of the balcony, the Doctor's screams faded away to nothing. Then all was quiet, until a little bird began to sing.

Pippin and Granny gasped – this was not what anyone had expected. Mungo was devastated that he had accidentally harmed the Doctor. 'I'm so sorry,' said the big man. 'I didn't mean to hurt him. I had no idea. I just wanted to stop him getting to Pippin . . .' He tailed off, big fat tears of salty sadness filling his eyes.

Granny and Pippin pulled him in for a

cuddle. 'Oh dear,' she said soothingly. 'It was not your fault, my love. He was on a bad path and I don't know what we are going to do. I don't think you will have done him any real harm.'

'He's got Jean's lives,' said Pippin, patting Mungo on the back. 'He will be back,' and she gave him an extra squeeze to let him know that she felt exactly the same way as her granny. 'Thank you for saving me,' she smiled, looking up at her lovely, big, favourite geologist-mayor mash-up.

Little Shiny Pippin looked at the spot where Doctor Blowfart had been standing. Something glistened on the floor. It was the golden key that the Doctor had made using Mungo's chain. As she picked it up she noticed something remarkable. Where the powerful chain had hit the wall, there was a small hand-sized hole.

'Hey, look at this!' she said, rushing over. Mungo peered inside. Then he began pulling brick after brick out from the wall, stacking them in a big pile. It wasn't long before he'd made a large-enough opening to step through. On the other side was a staircase which led up into the clouds, high above the temple.

'Granny, the prophecy!' said Pippin, and the old lady pulled out the ancient piece of paper.

And a lock which cannot be undone

By a simple key for the upstairs-

upstairs you will need

Golden drops one, two, three

'The key! It wasn't for the door the Doctor was trying, it's for the upstairs-upstairs! The word is joined, but your mum wrote it on

two lines! Do you see? The upstairs-upstairs is a place! Another *secret* upstairs *after* the very top floor!'

'You clever girl!' said Granny. 'Let's go. To the upstairs-upstairs!' In silence, the team stepped through the hole in

the wall and began to climb.
They soon reached the top, and
at the top found themselves on a landing
in front of four doors, each one marked
with a word: Everywhere, Adventure,
Eternity and Home.

Pippin looked at her granny. She spoke no words but her eyes said, *Well, can I?*

Granny raised an eyebrow, which Pippin knew meant, *If you think it's okay.*

The little girl nodded slowly, took the magical key and opened the first door, the one marked Everywhere.

Through the door was a sight that made them all stand back in amazement – a landscape with great pyramids rising up out of a desert and a pair of camels trekking through the sand.

Five hundred and nine jinkies, my lovely book friends, this is so amazoinks. I wish I was there with them, don't you? I feel so funusually excited and nice.

Pippin closed the door, not quite able to believe her big brown eyes. She pinched herself on the leg quite hard to make sure that she was not dreaming. Then she pinched Mungo to make sure HE was not dreaming.

'Ouch!' said the big man, who understood why he had been pinched. 'We can't both be dreaming,' he added, as Pippin opened the Everywhere door again very slowly.

This time she saw an icy landscape with polar bears and a sleepy village made of igloos. I feel as though I daren't write any more. It was incredibubble and

wonderskill. Pippin could not believe either of her eyeballs.

The little girl closed and then reopened the door one last time and saw a farmhouse in the mountains next to a huge crystal-clear lake. Everybody exchanged glances, speechless. Mungo bent down and picked his chin up off the floor.

Closing the door and carefully locking it, Pippin looked at Granny and the others, but there were no words that any of them could say about what they had just seen.

Granny raised her eyebrows towards the second door, the one that had Adventure written upon it. Using the key, Pippin opened it carefully and the team peered through.

They saw a canyon with cliffs and cactuses, and a fast-moving steam train full of people, and men on horseback galloping alongside the train.

'Woo-hoo!' said Mungo, getting excited. 'I want to go there and be a sheriff and chase bad cowboys on horseback and then sit around a campfire eating beans and farting.'

Pippin looked at the big man and smiled. 'Remember you are a mayor now, which definitely means less farting.' The little girl closed the Adventure door again and opened it a moment later to see that it led to the control centre of a space rocket that was just about to launch.

This was too much to take in. Pippin knew instinctively that there were an infinite number of possibilities behind each door. She also knew that to leave them unlocked would be very dangerous, so she locked this door just as carefully as the last one.

This adventure they were all on now felt so funbelievable that nobody knew quite what to say. Excitement crackled in the air as everybody prepared themselves for what the next door might hold.

Pippin unlocked the second-to-last door, the one marked Eternity. What she saw almost made her eyes pop out. Spread out before her was a huge train station from the olden days with people rushing to and fro. Granny turned and had to take a seat on a chair. 'I'm too old for this kind of nuttyness,' she announced, popping a podgy marshmallow in her mouth to give her some more funergy.

Pippin gazed for what seemed like hours at the unexpected scene spread out before her. Huge steam trains were snorting in a station. She saw a kiosk selling newspapers and cigarettes, and curled up on the counter lay a big creamy-coloured cat with a kind face. This was almost too much for the team to take in, and their hearts were beating fast. They all began to realise that they had a key for everywhere, for all of time and more.

Pippin looked at Granny. 'This is too much for now. I want to go home.'

'Me too,' agreed Mungo. 'My flabber has been completely gasted. I need five Cornettos, nine Magnums and a Fab.'

'Quite right,' replied Granny. 'I'm glad you said that. I'm zonk-a-doodle-clankered and what I need now is my sofa and some lovely snooker on the telly.'

'Woo-hoo. Me three,' said Mungo, with his chain around his neck.

And so Pippin unlocked the last door – Home. One by one, they approached the door and stepped through.

Pippin grinned from ear to ear! She was back on the other side of the impossible door in Granny's shed – the door from the beginning of this banging gladventure! The door that was absurd, preposterous, inconceivable and totally out of the question had turned out to be fantastic, marvellous and, in the end, really rather useful.

Each and every one of them breathed

a huge sigh of relief. What a time they'd had! But now they were back inside Granny's garden house with its smell of wood, lawn mowers, deckchairs and barbecue charcoal, on the right side of the impossibly fabulous door. They hugged and hugged until they were all hugged out, not quite believing what had happened to them all. They had just had the gladventure of a lifetime.

Phew

Very almost

NEARLY THE END

Zoinks

I feel so happy

Me too

That was a nutty badventure

Wasn't it

287

Wasn't it though?

X

Huge

Wowzers John Trousers. Just like lovely Granny, I feel zonk-a-doodle-clankered after that funusually terribubble badventure. I told you that it was a humdinger.

Outside in Granny's garden, Mungo said goodbye. With his now repaired magical mayoral chain around his neck, he was able to talk to Oddlop.

'Would you like me to walk you home, you amazing little green ninja?' said the big fella.

'I thought you'd never ask, *amigo*!' replied Oddplop with a grin. 'It is time for me to hop off home to my pad – my LILY pad.' The little green superstar sprang up onto Mungo's shoulder and with a wink and a wave to the others, they made their way off into the forest.

Granny and Pippin went inside and the little old lady put together a tray of delicious nonsense for them to snack on in front of the television. They had Monster Munch for their main course and marshmallows for pudding, all washed down with delicious fizzy lemonade, which as you lovely people know is most excellent for burping.

On the sofa, in between snacks, they chatted about their crazy adventure. Chasing the monkey burglars, the amazing island, Salty Judith . . .

'Gaah! What about Salty Judith?' asked Pippin.

'Oh, don't worry,' said Granny. 'I thought about that. I called her on the walkie-talkie and told her to take the chopper back to Gatacre's Cove. She'll be home by now with her very own stolen helicopter.'

Between the chattering and the nattering, Pippin began to look through Edward's diary, which was beside them on the sofa. It felt nice for Pippin to read the words of her great-uncle before he became naughty Doctor Blowfart. She wanted so much to bring him back from the bad side. The little girl turned the pages one by one, looking at Edward's drawings and reading about his trips. Towards the end of the book she let out an enormous gasp.

'Gasp,' she gasped. A photo of a cat had fallen out from the back of the book. 'Gran, look!' She turned the photo over and the word 'Jean' was written on the back.

'What is it?' asked Gran. 'That's just Jean, Edward's cat who died. What's wrong, my dear?'

'I saw that cat through one of the doors, in the the big olden-days station!' Pippin blurted. 'I did. I know it. I'm sure!'

Pippin and her granny held hands and looked at one another. They both knew that this was incredible news.

Jean was alive and this was fantastic. If they could find Jean, then *surely* they could bring Edward back for good and put an end to his naughtiness as evil Doctor Blowfart forever and ever. Granny and Pippin stared at each other. Neither knew quite what to say . . .

The End

Until Next Time

That is

Goodnight

Yes

Goodnight

HH

XXX

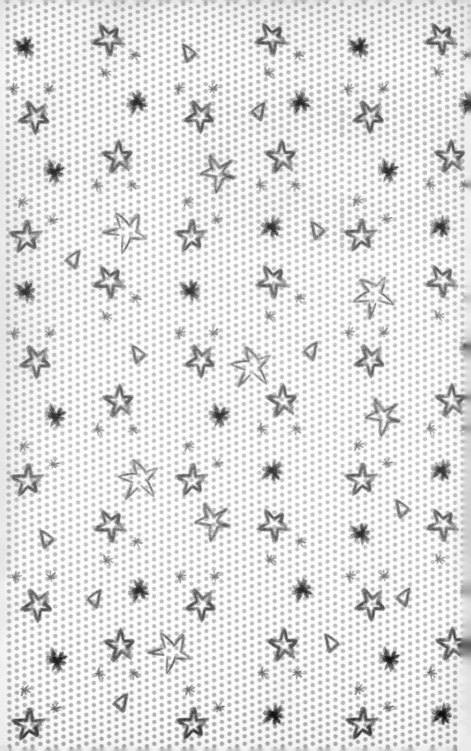